UNDER ABDUCTION

Andrew Neiderman

POCKET BOOKS

NEW YORK   LONDON   TORONTO   SYDNEY   SINGAPORE

This book is a work of fiction. Names, characters, places and incidents are products of the author's imagination or are used fictitiously. Any resemblance to actual events or locales or persons living or dead is entirely coincidental.

An *Original* Publication of POCKET BOOKS

 POCKET BOOKS, a division of Simon & Schuster, Inc.
1230 Avenue of the Americas, New York, NY 10020

ISBN: 0-7434-1269-9

First Pocket Books printing December 2002

10   9   8   7   6   5   4   3   2   1

POCKET and colophon are registered trademarks of Simon & Schuster, Inc.

For information regarding special discounts for bulk purchases, please contact Simon & Schuster Special Sales at 1-800-456-6798 or business@simonandschuster.com

Front cover illustration by John Vairo, Jr.; photo credits: Simon Rowe/Photonica, Ross Rappaport/Photonica, Jason Horowitz/GettyImages

Printed in the U.S.A.

*For the faculty of Fallsburg High,
alongside whom I spent some of
the best years of my life*

Prologue

Anna Gold stared at the telephone on her light maple wood secretary desk in the den as she slipped her left arm into her navy blue wool coat. She thought she could will the phone to ring, will her lover to follow through and, as he had promised, make her the most important person in his life. He should have called this morning to confirm their plans, all that they would do to make a future together, now that he knew she was pregnant with his child.

She had waited until after lunch to go for groceries because she didn't want to miss him, but here it was nearly one and he still hadn't called. In fact, no one had called this morning, and the silence of her solitude hung in the air of her apartment with a heaviness that resembled the aftermath of a funeral.

The lines were dead now between her and the

people she loved and the people who should love her. She had acquaintances, superficial friendships with girlfriends who were citizens of the same country of loneliness, young women about her age who were searching for some meaningful relationship too. Her work as a paralegal at the public defender's office had brought her into contact with many different kinds of people, but she had yet to find the close friend with whom she was comfortable enough to share intimacies—intimacies that, up until now, she had shared only with her sister. She had told no one except her lover and her sister that she was nearly two months pregnant. She had confirmed it herself with one of those home-test kits.

Almost immediately in a panic, she had made inquiries about having an abortion and had even gone so far as to have an appointment with Dr. Carla Williams at the Mountain Clinic. But then she had calmed down and thought, *If he loves me as much as he says he does and is ready to make this change in his life, why have an abortion?* She never even told him she had gone to find out about it. As far as he knew, that wasn't a choice, not with her religious background. And she was encouraged by the fact that he had never even suggested it.

Instead he had sat there with that same sweet smile on his face, his hazel eyes brightening when she had told him, and he had nodded and said, "Well, I guess this means we'll just have to move things along a little faster than I had anticipated.

Nothing to worry about. I'll be here for you; I'll always be here for you."

He brought her to tears when he added, "You've given me a new lease on life, just when I thought I had made tragic mistakes and buried myself in misery. Thank you, Anna. Thank you for being here," he told her, and they kissed.

But that had been days ago, and he hadn't called her this morning as he had promised.

She began to button her coat, her fingers trembling with the disappointment that filled her with an emptiness, a hollowness in her chest. The third button from the top on her coat dangled ominously on loose threads. Anna was not the homemaker her mother had been and her sister was; she couldn't mend clothing and she was, at best, a mediocre cook. Her mind had always been on what she considered more lofty endeavors. She wasn't going to be frustrated in her pursuit of a career and a more cosmopolitan life, no matter what her family's traditions were.

She would have been a full attorney by now if her father hadn't discouraged her and pulled back on the little support he had given her soon after her mother's death. The estrangement that followed was destined. She believed it was built into her genes: She had inherited her father's strong determination, and that, perhaps, was why they had been combatants for so long—they were too alike. Of course, her father would never admit to such a thing. She was merely rebellious, foolish, ungrateful. She couldn't have a sensible discussion with such a man.

Yet, his face haunted her at times like these. The vision of him furiously standing before her remained vivid. There were those big, dark eyes of his, tragic eyes that saw the world through shattered glasses. His shoulders, powerful though they were because of the work he did with stone, still always seemed sloped with the burden that followed two thousand years of persecution.

"You are like their Christ," she once accused, which brightened his face with the blood beneath his skin as she had never seen it brighten before. "You take all the misery onto yourself. You crucify yourself. Instead of nails in your hands, you pierce your soul with the pictures of the Holocaust or daily examples of anti-Semitism. You want me to march through endless cemeteries with you."

After the initial shock of her words, her father swelled, his shoulders moving up and back as if they were being pumped full of air, and he glared at her with that face of the prophets he often assumed and said, "You can run; you can hide. You can put a cross around your neck if you like, but you can never deny who you are and what you are."

Was he right? One of the things she had done when she first moved in here was put a mezuzah on the doorjamb. She couldn't help it. It just seemed natural and she wasn't ready to spit in the face of her faith. She simply wanted breathing room to become her own person. Was that such a terrible thing?

At the door of her apartment, she paused and glanced at the phone on the side table in the living room. That one didn't ring either. Of course, there was the answering machine, but her lover rarely left a message on it, and she knew that even if he did, she wouldn't be able to get back to him.

She hated herself for making herself so dependent on someone else's schedule, responsibilities, and whims. How had she grown after escaping the confinement in her father's house? Where was this precious freedom she had dreamt she would have?

"I'm still no better than a puppet, and this time I have no one to blame but myself," she muttered, and opened the door.

Her apartment was in one of the new complexes built outside of Monticello, New York, the biggest village in Sullivan County and the center of county government. These were advertised and sold as garden apartments, each with its own small balcony looking over the pool and landscaped commons. But being in upstate New York, the pool was utilized only between eight to ten weeks, if they were lucky, and during the long winter months, the flower beds were dead or brown, the bushes were thin, the walkways were usually streaked with mud, ice, or snow. Now the pool was an empty shell gathering debris.

Except for attending Yeshiva University in New York and spending a year at the Benjamin N. Cardozo School of Law, she had spent all of her twenty-six years in this area, the Catskill Mountains, once known as the Borscht Belt. But she was comfortable here and she could be on her own here; she still felt protected by familiarity. Setting out to start a new life in a completely new vicinity after cutting herself off from her father was too terrifying. Despite her need to be cosmopolitan, she was handicapped by her need for stability. It was part of the contradiction, the confusion of identity, that kept her searching for answers.

Did she, as she naggingly feared, grab too quickly on to someone else's affection?

She had fallen in love, depended on someone's promises, surrendered to passion and now—now she was in trouble because the clock was ticking. The magic of life, the making of a baby, had started. It wasn't something planned, but the impulsiveness with which she and her lover had begun their relationship permeated everything they did. Everything they did was on the spur of the moment, which made it even more exciting. She was tired of being the well-organized, sensible young woman.

One minute she was planning to make a cup of tea, read a book, and go to sleep, and the next moment she was rushing off to meet him at a motel or out-of-the-way bar and then a motel. It was wonderful to be taken by surprise, to defy what was sensible, to be carefree and throw caution over-board with the frenzy of one desperately trying to stay afloat.

Sometimes they would be riding along talking, and suddenly he would stop, pull into a side road, and they would be at each other. She had never known such passion. She had had crushes on boys, but never developed a real relationship with any-one, even at the university. Maybe she was inexpe-rienced and naive, more like an adolescent when it came to matters of the heart, but she truly believed her lover was just as taken with her as she was with him. In fact, he appeared to love her more for her simplicity and innocence. How many times had he told her she made him feel like a young man again, falling in love for the first time himself?

If all that is so true, Anna, why the delay? Let's get this life started, she thought. But now, with his hesitation, his hemming and hawing, his long list of excuses, she had grave doubts gnawing at her insides.

And so, to abort or not to abort, that was the question—the question of the age, it seemed; only now it was dreadfully a personal question. She had been impressed with Dr. Carla Williams. The head of the clinic had taken great pains not to influence her one way or the other.

"This has to be your sole decision, Anna," she had told her. "I just give you the facts. I'm not anyone's priest, minister, or rabbi. I have enough trouble looking after my own soul." Anna liked her. If she was going to have it done, Carla Williams was the sort of doctor she'd want doing it, she thought.

Anna knew what her sister, Miriam, had thought about it, but this wasn't happening to Miriam; it was happening to her. Miriam couldn't begin to understand, even though Miriam was older. Miriam was even more cloistered and inexperienced at matters of the heart than she was. Miriam could only gasp or exclaim or cry.

Well, she wasn't Miriam. She was her own person and she would make up her own mind. She vowed she would do whatever she had to do and be persuaded by nothing except her own feelings.

"Don't quote scripture at me, Miriam," she told her. "This is the real world I'm in."

But her bravado weakened when she gazed at the mezuzah in the doorway. Despite her protest, moral law weighed heavy on her conscience. Independence and finding her identity was one thing; defiance was another. She closed her eyes, kissed the tips of her fingers, and then opened her eyes and touched the mezuzah before walking out and closing the door behind her.

Anna moved quickly down the walkway toward the covered parking spaces. Each tenant had two, but she needed only one for her late-model Honda, which she had leased. Everything in her life was leased right now, including the furniture and the kitchen ware in the apartment. She had even rented her television set on a rent option to buy deal. At least she owned her clothes, some not-very-valuable jewelry, and the towels and linens.

When she had left home, she had little more than a thousand dollars, but she had the job and the promise of some sort of future doing work she felt gave her life more meaning. It was enough to give her the courage to be on her own, and so she had been for nearly a year, but now she was also in trouble.

Or was she? Perhaps he would fulfill his promises. Perhaps he was as deeply in love with her as she thought, hoped. If only he had called this morning, if only she had some concrete reason to be optimistic, if only . . .

She started the engine and drove the mile and a half to the supermarket. Saturday was supermarket day for her now, but it wasn't always. In fact, she never rode in a car on Saturdays, much less go shopping. As she drove through the quiet streets she envisioned her father's face again, his grimace, the dark way his eyes turned down because of the shameful burden she had become.

Even now, even after all this time and all she had done and said, she couldn't keep out the tiny pinpricks of guilt that stabbed her heart. It was as if God were looking down on this stupid supermarket parking lot and making notes in his divine notebook.

Anna Gold shopped and rode in her car on the

Sabbath, and after I had strictly told them all: Remember the Sabbath day and keep it holy. This is keeping it holy? Comparing prices, clipping coupons, squeezing fruit?

Anna laughed at her own imaginative deific dialogue. She didn't intend to be irreverent or blasphemous, but as she had told Miriam, she simply wasn't going to live in the Middle Ages, or even before the Middle Ages, which was how she characterized her father's faith. Her sister stood in the hallway of their house with her mouth agape as Anna vehemently espoused her beliefs the day she left.

"Religion has nothing in common with reality. One church still prohibits the use of condoms, even though a storm of dire disease, AIDS, rains down on humanity, while another prohibits sick children from getting the medicine they need or the blood transfusion they need. And we're no better with our archaic kosher laws and our fanatical adherence to the Sabbath. The world still turns on Saturday, Miriam!"

"Anna," she gasped, "God is listening."

"If He's listening," she said, "He must be hysterical with laughter watching these holy men twist and turn what He created into their own creations."

Her sister's face whitened. She looked to the living room where their father sat, fuming.

Poor Miriam, Anna thought; she hated leaving

her behind, but maybe that was where her sister would rather be, maybe that was where she belonged. They were sisters, but they really were two different people. Miriam wouldn't be caught dead pushing a cart down a supermarket aisle on Saturday. She would be afraid her hands would burn.

Anna smiled and shook her head at the thought as she moved along, pulling boxes rapidly from the shelves, pushing the cart down the aisle, nearly knocking over an elderly lady who was comparing prices. It wasn't that crowded, however, so she was able to get to a checkout counter sooner than she thought. She wanted to get home just in case he called. This was the weekend he was supposedly telling his wife. This was the weekend it would really begin for them. On Monday she would be able to walk with her head high and stop feeling like a sneak.

As she pushed her cart through the entrance of the supermarket and toward her car, she caught sight of a late-model Ford sedan parked to her left in a no-parking zone. The two people who sat up front, a young man and a young woman, were staring at her. The woman was at the wheel. Anna thought nothing of it until she paused at her car, opened her trunk, and turned to see the sedan come up the lot toward her. She put her pocketbook in the trunk and loaded in the first bag. But then she paused again when the Ford came to a stop right behind her.

The man stepped out quickly, a Model 10 Smith & Wesson .38 pistol clutched in his right hand. To Anna it looked like a cannon. She gasped at the sight of the gun: Her experience with weapons was practically nonexistent; in fact, she could count on her one hand how many times she had actually seen a gun in real life. She even hated seeing violence on television or in the movies and usually had her head down during those scenes. Some soldier in Israel she would make.

Anna held her breath, her right palm over her heart. A holdup in broad daylight? These things happened only to other people and rarely in this semirural, laid-back world miles and miles from urban centers. At least, that was what she had believed up to this moment.

Without saying anything, the man with the gun opened the side door of the car.

"Get in," he ordered. "Quickly."

Anna didn't move. It was enough of a shock to think she was being robbed, but what he demanded now turned her heart to stone and made her tremble so, she thought her teeth would soon begin to chatter. She shook her head. It was all she was capable of doing. If she tried to run, she was sure to stumble.

"Get in or I'll kill you right here," he said firmly. He had blue eyes that turned into glass. He looked younger than he apparently was; he had a baby face, soft cheeks, and thick red lips, but he looked hypnotized, crazed, far from an innocent, harmless child.

"Who are you? What is this?" she asked, and at the same time gazed around for someone to help her.

There was no one nearby. It was fall in the Catskills. Whatever tourists and summer visitors there had been were long gone, and the area had been returned to its small population of year-round residents. In some nearby hamlets a good twenty minutes could pass before a car would roll down Main Street.

There was a woman two rows down in the parking lot just getting out of a car with her little girl—hardly anyone to come to the rescue, Anna thought—and the people in front of the supermarket were too far away and too distracted to be of any assistance either.

"Last chance," the baby-faced man said, and pushed the barrel of the pistol into her stomach. His lips writhed and his eyes were full of purpose. There was no bluff to call here. "Get in," he ordered and pulled the front of her coat. The loose button popped off.

Terrified, Anna obeyed and got into the car. He slammed the door closed and got into the front. The female driver accelerated and they pulled out of the parking lot quickly, shooting up the street toward the main highway, New York Route 17.

"Who are you? What do you want?"

"Put your hands up here," he ordered in response.

He indicated the back of the seat. "Do it!" he shouted.

She did so and he quickly wrapped fishing line around her wrists to bind her. It was so tight that if she moved one hand an eighth of an inch, the fishing line cut into her skin. She grimaced and complained.

"It hurts!"

"Just for a little while," he said, smiling.

Who were these people? What did they want with her?

She gazed back at the fast-fading sight of the parking lot. The trunk of her leased automobile was still open, and most of her groceries were still in the cart.

A chill of terror tightened around her waist. It resembled the labor pains she anticipated would come. Her throat tightened, and tears came to her eyes.

The man turned around.

"Thank you for being cooperative, Anna," he said.

"Yes, thank you," the female driver parroted.

As they drove on, Anna was unable to see that they were looking forward with the same ecstatic smile on their faces, each reflecting the other's overwhelming sense of happiness.

1

The abortion clinic was under siege, surrounded. It looked like a scene from a B cowboy-and-Indian movie because it had been constructed about three miles out of the village and back a good five hundred yards from the highway. It resembled a wagon train, isolated, vulnerable, under attack.

There was a nicely maintained lawn in front of it, a small parking lot behind the wood building, and behind that was a field and woods. The building itself looked nothing like a medical structure. It seemed more like someone's home, a two-story Colonial revival with a simple entry porch, the whole building in a soft, Wedgwood blue, the windows with curtains and flower boxes. There were two wide redwood chairs and a small redwood settee on the front lawn.

It was at least a half mile to the next structure in any direction. The clinic had been deliberately placed where there would be a sense of privacy. The patients who came didn't feel under surveillance. Not until today, that is. Today the clinic was under attack.

Upwards of fifty members of the militant Shepherds of God surrounded the building and moved in a circle. They wore no special uniforms. Most of them looked like ordinary people, housewives, gentlemen. A few of the men even wore shirts and ties. Some of them waved welded iron crosses, a number of them ominously sharpened at all ends. About a dozen beat on tin drums. Most of the women carried dolls streaked with blood. All chanted, "Murder, murder, murder."

Dr. Carla Williams stood inside the front entrance, facing the closed front doors like the palace guard, her arms folded over her bosom. Her two patients, both women in their early twenties, hovered behind her in the lobby. Millie Whittaker, the fifty-two-year-old receptionist, was on the telephone, screaming hysterically at the state police dispatcher. Two nurses lingered in the examination-room doorway. All eyes were on Dr. Williams.

One of those porcelain dolls streaked with blood came through the front window and shattered on the tile floor, the shards of glass falling in and around it. Everyone except Dr. Williams screamed.

"Bastards," she muttered. She was thirty-eight, divorced, the mother of two girls, one ten, the other twelve. Despite her five feet six inches of height and

128 pounds, she presented a formidable appearance: determined, unmoved, resourcefully independent. She had become one of the area's most well known advocates of women's rights, appearing at many panel discussions and debates, and often as the guest speaker at dinners. She took on all opponents without discrimination: priests, rabbis, archconservatives, wishy-washy politicians.

Without warning the fanatical right-to-lifers had descended on her clinic. Usually a demonstration like this came only after bitter charges made in the media, well publicized so they would get more media coverage and attract an audience of sympathizers.

This morning, however, their cars just suddenly lined the highway and it appeared that more were coming. Carla saw them as moralistic locusts, religious demagogues who would have their way or else.

Suddenly a storm of rocks penetrated every window in the clinic.

"Back away!" Carla shouted.

Her two patients rushed out of the lobby and into the corridor, screaming. The nurses guided them to safer quarters.

"Where are the police?" Carla shouted.

"On their way," Millie cried. She lowered herself as a rock bounced off the counter.

"Murder, murder, murder . . ."

The circle was tightening. Their chanting grew

louder. More rocks were thrown. It had the effect of an earthquake shaking the very foundations of the building.

"They can't do this to me," Carla muttered. "This is America."

She had defeated a womanizing, degenerate of a husband in court despite his high-priced legal representation; she had built a lucrative practice, and she was successfully raising two children while maintaining an active medical career. A bunch of religious fanatics would not make her back away another inch. She had faced down these people many times before; she would do it again.

With a surge of courage, she seized the doorknob.

"Doctor Williams!" one of the nurses called.

"Stay back," she said. Carla stepped out on the small porch and the maddening circle slowed its tightening and shrinking. Rocks pelted the sides of the building and some kicked out the jagged pieces of glass that lingered in window frames, but even that came to an end in the face of this unexpected appearance.

"How dare you do this?" Carla screamed at the distorted faces of rage that faced her. They all looked like they wore the same mask. "There are people in here with families, just like the rest of you, and you are terrifying them and harming them. Where's your Christianity? You are violating laws, destroying property."

Some of the crowd wilted, but others simply stared. Carla walked down the steps and paused on the sidewalk to glare back at the protesters.

"I want you all off my property this moment, do you hear? Get off!"

She waved her fist at them.

"Move away!"

No one moved. Then the chanting started again, low at first, but building and building in volume and intensity: "Murder, murder, murder . . ."

Another rock was thrown and then another pounded the side of the building. One hit the porch floor.

Deep down in her gut, Carla felt a surge of fear that she hadn't felt since she was a little girl who had found herself alone on a dark night. All that was primeval in her being, her instinctive alarms, rang. Her organs cringed, her heart contracted, and her blood pounded and rushed from her head.

She was going to turn, back up, wait for the police, but without warning, seeming coming from the ground itself, one of those sharpened crosses flew into her chest, cracking the bone like brittle candy and slicing her heart in two. The last thing she heard was the distant, far-too-late sound of sirens before crumpling to the walkway, lowering the flag of life on her thirty-eight years, her medical education, her love for her children, her promising future.

Someone shouted, "Death to Satan!" and the crowd cheered.

Undaunted, they stood their ground and continued to chant, "Murder, murder, murder . . ." as the police began to arrive and rush from their vehicles: a cavalry that had come far too late to save this wagon train.

2

On the muted television screen, the Giants' offensive line took their positions on the five-yard line. It was third and goal. McShane leaned forward in his desk chair, hovering like some prehistoric man over the campfire. His shoulders were tense, firm, the lines in his face as etched and still as lines cut in granite. Although there was no sound on his nine-inch set because the sheriff didn't like it, McShane could hear the roar of the crowd in his memory, the excited voices of the commentators, and the recitation of the quarterback before the snap.

Just as the ball was flicked into the quarterback's hands, the phone rang. It pierced the moment and the quarterback was sacked.

McShane groaned. He believed in luck, and especially in the whimsy of chance. If that phone hadn't started ringing, the quarterback would have gotten off a goal-scoring pass. No question.

Now they would probably go for the field goal.

He seized the telephone receiver, squeezing the neck of it as if he could choke the voice out of the earpiece.

"McShane," he growled. Why wasn't the rest of the world watching the ball game? Why weren't criminals on a break?

"This is Harvey Nelson, manager of Van's Supermarket on Cranshaw."

"What can I do for you?" McShane asked, his eyes still glued to the silent set.

"We got a situation here. Someone left her Honda in the lot with the trunk open and the groceries still in the cart, exposed. One of my clerks found it when he helped someone else with her groceries. I went out there and we found the woman's pocketbook in the open trunk."

"Yeah?" McShane was only half-listening.

"We searched the pocketbook and found her wallet with her license. I've made announcements in the store and no one has responded."

"What's the name on the license?"

"Anna Gold. From her picture on the license, the clerk recalls her leaving. He didn't see her reenter the store and no one's seen her outside. Doesn't it look like something happened to her?" the manager whined when McShane didn't react to the news as dramatically as the manager had anticipated. "Why would she leave her car trunk wide open, her pocketbook visible, and groceries still in the cart like that, especially the refrigerated and frozen-food items?"

"Maybe there was an emergency and someone came to get her and she went home with them," he guessed. "Or she fainted and someone took her to the hospital."

Anything but a reason for him to have to leave, he pleaded with the gods.

"I didn't think about the hospital, but I've already called her home. We found her checkbook and her telephone number was on the check. All we got is an answering machine."

McShane groaned.

"What's the address on the license?"

"It's different from the address on her checkbook."

"You've really been looking into that pocketbook," McShane quipped.

"Well, it's . . . it's strange, just leaving all your things like that."

"All right. Give me the telephone number that's on the checks."

"I said I've already tried calling her home."

"Just give me the number anyway," McShane said. "Maybe she wasn't home yet. Maybe someone else is there by now."

There were at least a dozen *maybes* that would keep him in his seat in front of the television set. This was an important game and he had put money on the outcome.

"555-2121."

"Okay. I'll check it out and get back to you," he said, and cradled the phone just as the kicked ball sailed through the goalposts. They were still behind by four points. "I would have gone for it," he mumbled. "Everyone plays it safe."

For a moment he forgot what he was going to do. Then he dialed the number the supermarket manager had given him.

An answering machine picked up on the third ring and a sweet little voice asked him to leave name, time of the call, and number. He left nothing and instead pressed the button on his phone for the dispatcher.

"Mark, get me the Community General Hospital emergency room," he demanded.

There was a commercial break as the teams set up for the new kickoff. He drummed his fingers on his knee, impatient. The phone rang.

"Go ahead," Mark said.

"This is Detective McShane with the sheriff's office. Did you have a recent admittance by the name of Anna Gold by any chance?"

"No," the nurse replied. "We're actually having a quiet day, which everyone around here thinks is ominous."

"Right. Okay, thanks," he said, then replaced the phone and reluctantly got up and turned off the television set.

"Shit," he complained to no one in particular, and

started out of the sheriff's station. With the cutbacks in personnel and everyone else out in the field on one assignment or the other, he was the only one available to answer the call. The sheriff was at some meeting at the county office building. He was really the only one manning the fort.

As he passed Mark Ganner, the dispatcher, McShane lifted his hands in surrender.

"What's up, Jimmy?"

"I'm going over to Van's Supermarket to check out a deserted bag of groceries."

"Sounds like a convenient excuse to run away from an embarrassing loss on the football field," Mark quipped. "Didn't you have the Giants and six today?"

"Don't remind me," McShane said, and walked into the dreary overcast early afternoon.

Despite the gray skies, he slapped on his Ray-Bans before he crunched his six-foot-four-inch, 240-pound body behind the wheel. His sunglasses were tinted and made the dull world around him brighter. Before he put the transmission into drive, he fiddled with the radio dial. Unfortunately, the game was only on an AM station, so the commentator's remarks were surrounded with static and, at times, were buried in a gruesome interfering hum.

Just like his whole life, he thought, and accelerated through Main Street toward the shopping market just outside the village.

Just ahead of him, an ambulance burst out of the

building near the firehouse and turned up the street, its siren blaring.

"I wonder if that has anything to do with this," McShane mumbled and went faster, but the ambulance turned up the highway toward Port Jervis.

He shrugged, turned up the game, and continued toward the supermarket, thinking that emergency-room nurse would probably soon be sorry she had opened her mouth.

3

When they reached the Quickway entrance, they pulled to the side of the road and came to a stop.

Anna cringed in anticipation. What now? Other vehicles passed them, the drivers barely glancing their way. Suddenly a state police car rushed by, another right behind it. She thought about screaming but doubted they would hear, and besides, this man might just shoot her. He looked ready to do so back at the supermarket.

The young man stepped out after the second state police vehicle whipped past. He opened the rear door to slide in beside her. Then he plucked a black bandanna from his jacket pocket and dangled it in front of her.

"Sorry, but I have to put this on you now, Anna," he said, and wrapped the blindfold around her eyes, tying it snugly behind her head. She cringed and whimpered and then she sensed him leaning closer and closer until his lips were nearly caressing her earlobe. His hot breath was on her cheek.

"Nothing to worry about," he whispered. "God's in His heaven and all's well with the world."

His lips clicked against her cheek. It felt like he had snapped a rubber band. She pulled away with a gasp and he laughed.

"Ready?" the woman driver asked.

"Yes. We're all set here, aren't we, Anna?"

"Please," she said.

"It's all right. Try to relax."

His calm tone was more unnerving.

"I know," he followed. "We'll sing to pass the time."

"Good idea," the driver said.

"Ninety-nine baby bottles of milk on the wall, ninety-nine baby bottles of milk. If one of the bottles should happen to fall, ninety-eight baby bottles of milk on the wall."

The woman laughed.

"Come on, Anna," he urged. "Sing with us. It will pass the time. We have a little distance to go."

"Where are you taking me?"

"We're taking you to where you will be safe, and where the baby will be safe and be born," he replied.

How did they know she was pregnant? Her mind reeled. There must be a spy or some sort of informer at the clinic. Anna's sense of betrayal was superseded only by her sense of dread as the strange couple continued their singing.

"Ninety-eight baby bottles of milk on the wall, ninety-eight baby bottles of milk. If one of the bottles should happen to fall . . ."

He poked her in the ribs and she jumped.

"How many are left, Anna? How many bottles?" He poked her again. It hurt. She started to cry. "Anna?"

"Ninety-eight," she said quickly. Anything to get him away from her.

"No, Anna. Two have fallen. We started with ninety-nine. That leaves ninety-seven," he said. "If you sing along with us, you'll get it right the next time."

"That's right," the driver said.

"Come on, Anna, sing," he urged. He put his hand on her knee and squeezed. She tried to move away, but his grip was tight.

"You're hurting me," she complained.

"Don't hurt her," the driver ordered. "If you can help it," she added. "You know the condition she's in."

"I know."

He released Anna's knee.

"Sing along, Anna," he said.

Anna whimpered.

What's happening to me? Who are these people? Did anyone see them take me? she wondered.

His hand was on her shoulder now. It moved

slowly, in tiny increments, under her coat, down
her chest, and over her breast. He cupped it and
moved his hand up and down as if to weigh it. She
tried to slide away, but she was already near the
end of the seat. His other hand cupped her other
breast and he did the same thing. She tried to push
him away.

"Stop, Anna," he ordered, and brought his face
close to hers again, "or I'll put my tongue in your
ear."

She tried to swallow. It was getting harder and
harder to breathe.

"I know," he suddenly said, pulling his lips away
but keeping his hand on her breast. "I have a new
song to sing."

"What new song?" the driver asked.

He sang.

*"Oh, you gotta make milk, gallons and gallons of
milk. When the chips are saying you'll never feed,
you've got to make milk."* He paused. "How's that?"

The driver laughed.

"I like it. You know, breast-fed babies are the
healthiest babies."

"It's natural; it's what should be," he said. "Don't
you agree with us, Anna?"

She was hyperventilating now. The sweat had
broken out on her brow and her mouth was so dry,
she could barely swallow, and only with great effort.

Suddenly he wiped her forehead with a hand-
kerchief.

"Take it easy, Anna," he said softly. "We want you to relax and we prefer not giving you any medications until it's absolutely necessary, okay?"

"I don't have any money," she said, her voice cracking as her throat tightened.

"Did you hear that?"

"Yes," the driver said. She shook her head.

"It's all right, Anna. We aren't looking for any money. What we do is all for free," he added.

The driver laughed again.

"We're a nonprofit organization," she said.

"Supported by contributions," he followed. She laughed again.

"What is it you want? Please, tell me," Anna pleaded. The blindfold absorbed her tears.

"We want you to give birth to a happy, healthy baby," he said. And then he added, "Our baby. He or she is our baby because you don't want him or her, Anna. We can't let you get rid of our baby, now, can we?"

"I'm not getting rid of my baby," she said.

"Right. And the pope's not Polish."

"Watch your tongue," the driver snapped.

"Sorry."

"Where are you taking me? Please," Anna begged.

"We're taking you to the maternity wing," he replied. "All you have to do is give birth to a healthy baby, Anna. That's all we ask."

"But I'm barely two months pregnant," she said.

"Then we'll be getting to know each other really well, won't we, Anna? And you'll see how nice we can be."

"We can be nice," the driver interjected, "or . . ."

"Or not," he said. "Right, Mommy?"

"Right, Daddy," the driver replied.

Mommy? Daddy? Anna cringed.

His hand was on her shoulder again.

"Sing," he whispered. *"Ninety-seven baby bottles of milk on the wall, ninety-seven baby bottles of milk. If one of the bottles should happen to fall . . ."* He squeezed her arm. "Sing."

She started to sing.

"Ninety-six baby bottles of milk on the wall."

"Right. Good."

The driver laughed.

"That's wonderful," she called out.

They were all singing.

"Ninety-six baby bottles of milk on the wall . . ."

They rode on.

4

McShane made a sharp right when he entered the supermarket parking lot. The Giants were down to two minutes and still behind four points. It put him in a particularly bad mood, and he wasn't the sort of man who covered up his feelings well. Cookie always said he had a face a blind man could read.

A small crowd of the curious was gathered near the late-model Honda and the cart of groceries. He pulled up beside them and stepped out of his vehicle into the darkening Catskill Mountain afternoon. Up until now it had been an unusual fall in the upstate New York mountains. Temperatures were closer to summer highs, but McShane could literally smell winter in the air: There were no flowery aromas, no scents of newly cut lawns. Instead he smelled the heavier odor of rotting leaves, and the insides of his nostrils already stung with the impending Arctic-like air.

McShane removed his sunglasses. With his height and weight he was an impressive-looking man, trim and athletic, with piercing green eyes, dark brown hair, a firm mouth sliced across a powerfully full jaw, the bones of which became practically embossed in his skin when something made him tense.

Everyone turned to him. A young blond man in his mid-twenties wearing a Van's Supermarket apron moved forward first.

"Are you the police?"

"The whole division," McShane replied. "You Harvey Nelson?"

"No, *I* am," a chubby, bald-headed man with a Groucho Marx mustache said. He wore a white shirt, black tie, and black slacks. "Did you find out anything else? Was she taken to the hospital?"

"No."

McShane walked over to the cart. He gazed in it and saw the defrosting frozen foods, the two bottles of milk, and a container of cottage cheese. Obviously not the sort of foods someone would leave long. He turned. All eyes were still on him as if he would magically produce the woman or had the solution to the mystery at his fingertips.

"You say you made announcements in the store?" he asked the manager.

"Yes, about four times. We even checked the employee bathrooms."

McShane nodded and tried the driver's door. It was locked. The passenger side door was locked as well.

"Her keys are still in the trunk lock," the supermarket clerk said. "I didn't want to touch them."

McShane looked up and then sauntered back, self-conscious about the fact that he hadn't noticed.

He pulled them out quickly and then looked across the way at a small shopping mall.

"Anyone check over there?"

"She wouldn't leave her groceries like this and go shopping for something else," the blond clerk said.

"People do weird things," McShane replied. He hated know-it-alls at crime scenes.

"Yeah, but she didn't do that."

"How do you know that, Dick Tracy?"

"Her pocketbook," he reminded him. "It was there in the trunk when I looked. And she left all the frozen foods out here, and her milk."

McShane smirked. Everyone was a halfway-decent detective these days. It was because of all those television shows like *Murder, She Wrote*. All the mystery and glamour in his profession was gone. Every Tom, Dick, and Harry thought he could be Sam Spade or Philip Marlowe. That's what Columbo did to the profession, he concluded sadly.

"What happened to her?" a short, elderly lady

asked, a clear note of hysteria in her voice. She clung to her own pocketbook, pressing it to her breasts. "And in the parking lot in broad daylight? You're going to have to put a security guard out here," she told the manager.

"Easy," McShane said. "We don't know that anything bad has happened to her yet. Let's not jump to conclusions and get everyone upset," he warned the woman.

"There's still money in the pocketbook, so nobody robbed her," the supermarket clerk added, to help calm things.

McShane raised his amber eyebrows.

"Where is the pocketbook now?"

"Right here," the manager said, and bent down to pick it up. He had placed it next to the vehicle. It was a black imitation-leather bag.

"I didn't take anything out of it," the young man added quickly.

"I'll vouch for that," Harvey Nelson said. "I was here the whole time."

"Good," McShane said. "We always need reliable witnesses." He looked at the clerk. "What else did you touch?"

"Nothing. I just looked in the car to see if she had fainted or something."

McShane dipped his hand into the purse and came up with the wallet. There was a little more than forty dollars in it. Also in the purse he found lipstick, another set of keys, a book of matches from The Underground Bar in Port Jervis, a compact of cake makeup with an embossed Jewish star on the outside, and a hairbrush. There was some small change as well.

"Anyone see anything unusual?"

"No one," Harvey said. "We've already asked other customers. These people just arrived," he added, indicating the small crowd.

"Anyone here know the woman who owns this vehicle?" McShane asked. He looked at the license. "Anna Gold?" He held up the license so everyone could get a good look at the picture. People gaped, but all heads shook. "Okay. You might as well take the groceries back to the store," he told Nelson. "I'll see to the car," he added.

"What could have happened?" Harvey asked him.

McShane thought a moment.

"Aliens, maybe. It's too soon to tell," he said.

He started toward his vehicle but paused to pick up a button. He twirled it between his thumb and forefinger and then turned to the clerk.

"You waited on her?"

"Yes, sir."

"What was she wearing?"

"I just remember she was wearing a dark blue coat and seemed to be in a terrible hurry. When I had to have an item checked, she just said forget it."

"Uh-huh." He held up the button. "Look like one of the buttons from that coat?" McShane asked. The clerk shrugged.

"Could be. I don't look at the customers that closely," he added, more for the manager's benefit than McShane's.

McShane nodded and put the button in his pocket. He continued to his car, threw the purse on the seat, and reached in for the radio phone. Before he could flick it on, the dispatcher came through to ask all available personnel to go to the Mountain Clinic on Route 55, just out of Monticello.

"What's up, Mark?"

"A protest turned into a riot. State police have called for assistance. Looks like a doctor's down too."

"Great. Look, I need a tow truck at Van's lot. Looks like something suspicious. Late-model white Honda. Tell him to ask for the manager so he doesn't tow the wrong car out of here. Tell him to try not to touch the car too much and bring it to our lot."

"Gotcha."

"The sheriff back yet?"

"He's on his way to the clinic."

"Okay, so am I."

McShane started the engine and pulled away quickly, leaving the supermarket manager, his stock boy, and the small crowd staring after him. When he reached the exit, he slapped on his bubble light and hit his siren. The screaming alarm trailed behind his vehicle like a streamer. Vehicles parted to clear a way for him at the traffic light.

He was a little more than two weeks into a marital crisis, separated from his wife, with more scratching and clawing to come. Some of the clawing, maybe most of it, he would do to himself. He wasn't feeling particularly wronged, and try as he could, he couldn't find the blame to paint over Cookie and alleviate his own guilt. She methodically pointed out how he had mistreated her in small ways that accumulated into small mountains. She charged him with taking her for granted and ignoring and being insensitive to her needs—indeed, not just her needs but the needs of their marriage.

No new expression of remorse would help. He had tried throwing himself on the mercy of her court, but she was fed up, disgusted, emotionally bankrupt. She said if she was going to cry over him anymore, she would have to go to the sorrow bank and borrow tears.

"You were too young for any sort of real commitment, Jimmy, and I was too young to realize it," she analyzed. She spoke with a tone of fatality that put a chunk of cement in his stomach.

But all of this passed through his mind in a matter of seconds and was gone.

He was being a detective now and he had no partner of lower rank to assign his responsibilities while he went off and cried in his beer. He was alone at home and alone at the job. No one took his side and no one had much sympathy for him, not even his own parents or his brother. He didn't even have sympathy for himself, and right now he didn't have time to dwell on what was happening.

"Riot at the abortion clinic, doctor down, woman missing from her car in a supermarket parking lot, and the Giants were four points behind with seconds to play in the last quarter," he muttered. It was enough to make someone forget his own name, to say nothing of his own problems.

No wonder his soon-to-become-ex-wife of five years thought he was distracted from their marriage.

5

They seemed to be riding forever. She felt them make many turns and she heard the heavy traffic. Then, after a wide turn, she hardly heard any other cars. Their bizarre singing had also stopped, and the strange couple barely spoke to each other. The car bounced on what was clearly an old road, maybe even a dirt road.

The driver turned on the radio and dialed to a news station. They heard the bulletin about the abortion clinic and the death of Dr. Carla Williams. The commentator said more than twenty-five people, all members of Shepherds for God, had been rounded up and taken to the county jail. News reporters were already converging on the semirural community. By the evening news it would be infamous.

"Looks like we have something else to celebrate, don't we, Mommy?"

"Yes, we do, Daddy," the driver replied.

Dr. Williams was killed in a protest at about the same time she had been kidnapped, Anna thought. It looked like some grand conspiracy in which she had been caught. Despite her feeling, it couldn't be any worse; the terror had just been turned up another notch. Her heart was beating so hard, she thought it would simply burst, and she had more trouble catching her breath. Every once in a while she felt her face drain of blood. She told herself she had to battle to stay conscious. She was afraid of what they might do to her if she passed out.

Against the blackness of the blindfold, she could see her father's face full of pain when she had ripped herself out of his life. Her older sister, Miriam, would continue to cook and keep the house as she had since the death of their mother, who had felt guilty for becoming too sick to be a good wife, blaming herself for her own passing. It was another thing for which Anna couldn't forgive her father, even though he had never done anything or said anything to support her mother's guilt. It was his fault simply for being an Old World man.

Now she couldn't help but moan for her daddy. This kidnapping had turned her into a little girl again.

Anna felt them slow down and the car swing into a driveway. She heard the tires crackle over the gravel and felt them come to a stop.

"Where are we?" she asked.

"We're home," he said. "And at the maternity ward." He opened the door. Then he came around and opened the door on her side. He reached in and seized her at the elbow. "Step out slowly, Anna. We don't want you to fall. No more miscarriages at our birthing center, right, Mommy?"

"No more miscarriages."

More? What did they mean by *more?*

She felt the gravel under her feet as he led her over the driveway. There was some sort of monotonous grinding noise coming from somewhere on her right. She smelled the pungent aroma of damp earth and thought she heard the sound of a stream or brook. Then she heard a door being opened.

"Should I take off her blindfold now, Mommy? It would make it easier."

"One more moment," the woman replied. "Help her along, Daddy."

"Right. Anna, you're stepping down a stairway. Careful. Slowly."

She didn't want to move, but he was pulling her forward and she felt as if she were dangling. If she didn't move, he would release her and she would fall forward blindly. His foot guided her foot, keeping her on the steps.

"That's it. One more. Good. One more. Good."

"Okay, Daddy. Take it off now," the woman ordered.

She felt the blindfold being untied, and when she opened her eyes she saw that she was descending a chipped cement stairway to a basement door made of thick, weathered oak. The foundation of the building was constructed of fieldstone.

She tried to turn around to learn more about her surroundings, but he grabbed her head between his two hands and held it tightly, forcing her to face straight ahead.

"Don't look back," he warned. "You'll turn into a pillar of salt. Keep your eyes straight ahead. Go on. Continue walking," he ordered. There were two more steps to go.

"Why are you doing this? Please. I'll get some money for you."

"Walk, Anna, or I'll have Daddy carry you," the woman threatened.

She took the next step and then the next. The woman went ahead and inserted a key in the lock on the door. She pulled it open and entered ahead of them, turning on a light. A moment later Anna entered the basement and was greeted with a dank, musty odor. She was quickly brought to another door. Again a lock was undone, and she was led into a bedroom. There was a door on the far right through which she could see a bathroom. The basement bedroom had no windows. It had cement walls, painted bone white. The floor was carpeted with a tight light-brown rug. All the furniture in the room was eclectic: Nothing matched. There was a

light maple four-drawer dresser to the right of a dark
pine bed. On the left side of the room there was a
dark maple desk. Just to the right of the door was
an entertainment center with a nineteen-inch television set and a VCR beneath it.

The bed had a blue-and-white comforter and
matching blue-and-white pillows.

"Isn't this comfy-cozy?" the man said. "We'll
bring you books and magazines. There's a remote
on your nightstand next to the bed for the television set. No outside channels, I'm afraid: too much
pornography. There's a video deck under the television and we'll bring you videos from time to
time, and pamphlets. There are lots of things for
you to know, now that you're pregnant, aren't
there, Mommy?"

"Lots," the woman said.

The man stepped ahead to where there was a
chain coiled near the wall. When he picked it up,
Anna saw a metal collar attached to the end of it.
The other end was embedded in the wall. Anna
instinctively cringed as he approached with the
chain in hand, the links unfolding. She shook her
head and backed away, but the woman was right
behind her.

"Now, this is nothing. It's just our insurance pol-
icy on you. It won't hurt and you'll be free to move
about the room and use the bathroom at will," he
said, sounding like a kind doctor alleviating his
patient's fears.

She shook her head.

"No, please. Let me go."

"Mommy," he said, and the woman grabbed Anna's right arm above the elbow and squeezed with surprising strength.

Anna turned and looked into her eyes. She really hadn't looked at either of them very much: She had been too terrified. This woman didn't look to be more than thirty, if that. She had cold green eyes, a long nose with wide nostrils, and a thin mouth. Her dark brown hair hung limply over her ears and halfway down the back of her neck. Her forehead was peppered with pockmarks and there was a short but thick scar on her right cheek. She squeezed again, her fingers reaching bone, and brought her face close to Anna's.

"Don't be a bad mommy person," she advised. Anna felt the woman's nails digging through the sleeve of her coat. She tried to pull her arm out of the woman's grip, but it was like being caught in a pair of pliers. She stopped resisting and the woman eased her pressure. "Stand perfectly still," she ordered.

The man went behind Anna and snapped the thick metal collar around her neck. She heard it lock and felt the cold metal on her skin.

"Perfect," the woman said, gently pulling the collar up and down Anna's neck. "It's not too tight."

The man came around and cut the wire off

Anna's wrists. The blood rushed back to her numbed fingers.

"I'll get her ready now, Daddy," the woman said to the man. "Go lock the outside door."

"Yes, Mommy."

He turned and left the room.

"Take off your clothes," the woman ordered. "Quickly." She went to the dresser and opened the top drawer. Anna shivered. She was taking tiny breaths now. The weight of the metal collar on her neck seemed oppressive despite what the woman had said about it.

What happened next was beyond her control: She couldn't help it; she couldn't stop it.

Without any warning she started to scream, a long, piercing, desperate scream.

The woman turned and watched her for a moment, her face expressionless, perhaps even evincing boredom. Then she casually went to the bed, picked up the television remote, and clicked on the set and then the VCR. There was a tape already inserted. As the tape began to play she turned up the volume on a religious program so that it drowned out Anna's scream. After that, she returned to the dresser and plucked a nightgown out of the drawer.

Anna's voice gave out; she gasped for breath and stared as the woman approached. The evangelistic preacher on the television set was screaming, "Praise God! Praise God!"

"The quicker you get into your nightie, the quicker I can go prepare your supper and you can relax," the woman told her.

Anna shook her head.

The woman slapped her face so hard and so quickly, it seemed to come from the air. The crack turned her head and her face stung. Before she could respond, the woman hit her with her left hand on the other cheek, snapping her head around the other way.

"Praise God Almighty! Praise!" the television audience recited.

Anna raised her arms to protect herself from another blow. The woman grabbed her wrists and pulled her arms down and brought her face up to Anna's, so closely that Anna could feel her hot breath on her own lips.

"Take off all your clothes," she snarled, "and behave yourself. This is no way for a mother-to-be to act. Do it!" She threw Anna's arms back and Anna reluctantly, sniveling and gasping, began to disrobe.

"Good. Now that's more like it."

She pointed the remote at the set and turned down the television sound.

"We're all going to get along just fine. I knew it."

Anna stood naked, her arms over her breasts.

"Put on your nightie," the woman ordered. As she did so, the woman gathered Anna's clothing into a ball. "There are your slippers," she said, with a nod of her head toward the side of the bed. "I'll go now and get your dinner prepared. Just relax. I know it's been a bit of a difficult trip."

"Please," Anna said in a whisper. "My family will worry about me."

"What family? *We* are your family," the woman said. "You know that, Anna." She smiled and then she went to the doorway. After she opened the door, she turned back to smile again.

"Welcome, Anna. Welcome to your new home and our birthing center," she said and left, closing the door behind her.

The evangelist droned on with his audience cheering and clapping in the background.

6

The sheriff's station was bedlam. All the holding space and then some was filled with the Shepherds of God. State police, state investigators, and most of the local police on duty were there. Media people were crowding around the doorways and mingling in the parking lot. People were shouting questions, orders. Phones were ringing, radios cracking.

Ralph Cutler, the sheriff, was in his office, his normally red-tinged cheeks an absolute scarlet. At fifty-seven he was hovering around retirement. His daydreams were filled with clear-running mountain streams stocked with trout. In these dreams the only sounds were the murmurs of the brook, the singing of birds, and the whir of his fishing reel. It was quite a contrast to the cacophony of hysteria that now raged around him.

Ralph stood five feet ten with a small paunch that just poured over his wide black leather belt.

He had curly dark brown hair, bushy eyebrows that looked like patches of steel wool pasted over his hazel eyes, and a shiny, bulbous nose. His mouth worked nervously at the corners, even when he was just listening, as he was now.

The state police investigator was describing what forensics had done with the sharpened cross that had shattered Carla Williams's breastbone and sliced her heart. Fingerprints were being lifted from the cross even as they spoke.

"I want every one of those people fingerprinted," said the state police investigator, a tall man with a military-style haircut who was pumping the air with his puffy right forefinger. "We'll find out who threw the damn thing and charge the rest of them as accessories to murder. We've got to be careful here," he added, and lowered his voice to say, "This is politically charged. I've already had a call from the governor's office. Your county's going to be on prime-time national news."

"Thanks for the encouragement," Ralph said, and flopped into the worn imitation-leather chair behind his desk. The padding had long ago taken the shape of his buttocks. This was where his hemorrhoids had been born. He was as at home in the chair as a bird in its nest.

Through his glass door Ralph saw McShane pacing like a member of the immediate family outside the operating room. Periodically the burly detective raised his head and fixed his eyes in

Ralph's direction. Ralph knew he had something on his mind, some complaint, some request. "Take a number," he mumbled.

The phone rang. It was for the state investigator. Ralph handed him the receiver and then went to the office doorway. "What?" he asked McShane.

"I got something else brewing," McShane said. "Woman disappeared in the Van's Supermarket parking lot, left her groceries in the cart, car trunk open, her purse in the trunk, keys in the trunk lock, no sign of her at her home or at the hospital, and no one saw her leave the lot or anything unusual take place."

"Christ, like we don't have enough to do here," Ralph said, looking out at the commotion.

"I just need you to tell me which way to go," McShane said. "Stay here and help with this disaster or investigate this disappearance?"

"You sure this woman's really missing?"

"It's been about four hours," he replied after glancing at his watch. "I had to have her car towed off and still no word of her. Who the hell walks off, leaving their groceries and pocketbook like that?" He plucked the button from his pocket. "Found this at the scene. Might be off her coat. It could be some sort of forced abduction."

"Family?"

"Except to call her place and get an answering machine, I haven't done anything more than what

I just told you. I tried to tell you about it at the clinic, but you were occupied."

Ralph raised his eyebrows.

"Occupied," he muttered. Then he thought a moment. "Okay, run it down and get back here as soon as you can. The state guys are taking everything over, but I'd like to pretend we still have some responsibility and," he added, "ability. There's a lot of media here and a lot on the way. If it is a kidnapping, I'll call Reynolds at the FBI office."

"Right," McShane said, smiling. In a bizarre way he was grateful for the woman's disappearance: It got him away from this horrible mess. He hurried out of the station before Ralph Cutler changed his mind.

He decided to follow the address on the checkbook and make that his first stop. He was familiar with the relatively new apartment complex and knew where the manager's apartment was located. It was on the first floor, east of the pool. The name on the door read TOM ERNST. He pushed the buzzer and waited. A very thin woman who looked at least ten years older than her actual age came to the door in a faded pink robe. She gazed out at him with glazed, tired eyes. A cigarette emitted a stream of smoke that appeared to be going directly up her nostrils, but she didn't seem to mind. She looked as if she ate smoke for breakfast.

She squinted, even in the dull daylight, and removed the cigarette from her mouth.

"Tom's not here," she said before he could ask anything. "He's at the plumbing supply store, getting some toilet guts for an apartment."

McShane showed his ID. It straightened her posture but didn't bring any more life to her hazy eyes.

"You know Anna Gold in 216?" he asked.

"I don't know her. I know *of* her," she corrected. "Tom speaks to her once in a while. What she do?"

"She didn't do anything. I need to find out about her, though. She seems to be missing. Left her car open in the supermarket earlier today, groceries still in the cart. Have you seen her by any chance?"

"Ain't seen anyone today," she replied, "except Tom and now you."

McShane nodded as if he understood why she would stay locked away from people.

"Do you know how long she's been living here?"

"About a year, I think," she said.

"Do you know if she lives with anyone?"

"Don't know for sure, but she rented alone, I know that. I think she's a lawyer or works with a lawyer. Won't swear to it, though. You better wait for my husband if you want to know anything for sure."

She looked as though she were going to step back and invite him in, but McShane had other ideas, and the prospect of waiting for the woman's husband in that clammy apartment with this perfect model for every sort of "Before" shot was not inviting.

"I'll stop back," he said. She shrugged.

"Suit yourself," she replied, stuck the cigarette back into the corner of her lips, and closed the door.

McShane located 216 and dug into his pocket for the set of keys he had found in Anna Gold's pocketbook. As he had anticipated, one opened the door.

"Hello?" he called. He waited, listened for a response, and then entered. *With my luck, she's not missing*, he thought. *It's some sort of mix-up and I'll be held accountable for an illegal entry.* The possibility caused him to move tentatively into the small apartment.

It had the look of transience, sparse, with little identity. There were no pictures on the walls, no framed pictures of family or friends on shelves. In fact, it had the feel of a hotel room. *Anyone could be living here*, he concluded as he stood and perused the claustrophobic living room with its thin gray rug.

He glanced through the kitchen door. A plate and a cup and saucer were on the counter. He checked it out. The residue in the coffee cup was cold. What looked like the crumbs of some sandwich were on the plate.

He opened the refrigerator. You could tell a great

deal about someone from what was in his or her refrigerator, he thought, playing Sherlock Holmes. Did the person rely on fast food? Was there more food than a single person needed? Did he or she like rich things, care about fat content, eat vegetarian? You could tell immediately if there was a child living or often visiting. This refrigerator said little because there wasn't much in it. *Elementary stupidity, Watson. After all, where had she gone? To the supermarket, right?* he told himself.

He went through the living room and into the bedroom. He looked into the bathroom, opened the medicine cabinet, and noted that the products were all for a female. Also, there was only one toothbrush.

She lives alone and has no frequent male visitor, he concluded. He returned to the bedroom and opened a closet. Clothes were there; nothing to indicate someone was planning on leaving. *Who would leave like this anyway: just desert her car and groceries? Only someone who wanted you to think they were abducted, maybe. That makes a lot of sense, Sherlock. Maybe the supermarket clerk oughta be doing the investigating,* he thought, and laughed at himself.

He went to the secretary desk and started to sift through the mail. All he found were the usual utility and credit card bills, no letters, no notes.

He told himself this was the most anonymous person he had ever investigated. The dresser drawers contained nothing more than the basic clothing items. The jewelry was not very expensive-looking and the closet had nothing to knock your eyes out. In fact, McShane thought, this was a pretty simple, if not pathetic, wardrobe. He saw only two pair of shoes and a pair of sneakers.

The driver's license had indicated Anna Gold was twenty-six, old enough for someone to have been on her own for a while. *Teenagers accumulate more than this. Wherever she came from,* he thought, *she didn't bring much along.*

Where did she come from?

He took out the wallet and sifted through it, noting what the supermarket manager had told him: The address on the driver's license was different from the address on the checks. There was a Parksville address on the driver's license. Parksville was a hamlet outside of Liberty, so if it was her previous address, it wasn't too far away.

He started back through the living room and paused when he saw the light on the answering machine blinking. He pressed PLAY and waited. Whoever had called first had left no message, but there was a second message.

"Hi, Anna. I was just wondering if you were going to do anything special tonight or, should I say, see anyone special?" A short laugh was followed with "If not, call me and maybe we'll do something. Toby told me The Pit's been rocking. Lots of new hunks. I'll be home all afternoon. Oh," she added with a giggle, "just in case you don't recognize my voice: This is Lidia. Bye."

There were no other messages. McShane returned to the secretary's desk in the bedroom and searched the drawers. He didn't find a Rolodex, but he found a small pile of index cards with names, numbers, and addresses. One had Lidia Ambrook's number and address on it. He took the card and put it in his pocket, then flipped through the remaining cards. He really couldn't tell anything from the other names and addresses, but one card caught his attention because it had only a telephone number on it. He recognized it as a cellular phone number too. Instinctively he took that card out and put it in his pocket as well.

He gazed around the apartment once more and started to leave. Just before closing the door, however, he saw the mezuzah on the doorjamb. He had seen them before in the homes of Jewish people and knew that it contained some scroll and had holy significance. Yet, there was nothing else in this apartment to indicate it belonged to a religious person. He did recall the Jewish star on the compact case in her wallet.

He shrugged to himself and closed the door. As he backed away he heard someone say, "What the hell are you doing?"

He turned to see a tall, wiry man with disheveled black hair and a narrow face come walking toward him. He carried a small tool chest and a shopping bag and wore only a flannel shirt and dungarees despite the nippy, dank weather.

McShane flashed his ID.

"I know who you are," Tom Ernst said. "Wife told me you was snooping about. How'd you get into that apartment?" he asked, nodding at Anna's door.

"Key," McShane said holding up the key chain. "You're Ernst?"

"Yeah."

"The woman who lives here is apparently missing and might even have been abducted. What can you tell me about her?"

Ernst put his tool chest and the bag down.

"Nice lady. Lives alone. She works for the public defender's office. What do you mean, missing?"

McShane described the scene at the supermarket and what had followed.

"This is strange," Ernst said, scratching his head.

"Uh-huh. Any boyfriends, relatives you notice coming around?"

"I ain't never seen a man with her. Sometimes I seen another young woman. I don't snoop as long as they pay the rent on time and don't do damage, but I know she's got family in Parksville."

"Uh-huh."

"But I don't think they get along," Ernst added quickly.

"How do you know that?"

"She don't like talking about them."

"Oh?"

"I don't snoop—just read between the lines is all," he said defensively, and picked up his tool kit and the bag again. "I hope nothing bad's happened to her."

"Me too."

"Gotta fix a toilet down here. The old lady who lives in it will call me anytime, night or day, if I don't," he griped. McShane smiled.

"I'll get back to you," he said. "In the meantime, if she shows up, do me a favor and give me a call," McShane said, and handed one of his cards to Ernst. Ernst took it, nodded, and walked off.

McShane thought a moment and then started down the steps. Gold shouldn't be too hard a name to locate in Parksville, he thought. The whole hamlet probably didn't have a thousand people in it. *That's the nice thing about being a police detective in this area: There's usually only a small group of the usual suspects to round up.*

At least, that's the way it's been until now, he thought, and moved deeper into what he believed was becoming an increasingly ominous situation.

7

Anna sat on the bed and gazed at the stark white wall. The absence of color, the events, and the shock put her into a daze. She had her arms wrapped around herself, her hands clutching her shoulders. The woolen light-blue nightie was at least two sizes too big and draped her body without any style or shape, not that she cared. It was just that it did little to counter her feeling of total exposure. Her nudity beneath made her feel even more vulnerable, helpless.

Aside from what was now the muffled sound of that strange grinding noise from somewhere beyond the wall, it was relatively silent. Somewhere above her, the ceiling creaked. Occasionally she heard what sounded like water running through a pipe, and once she thought she heard a muffled voice, but the loudest noise by far was the sound of her own heavy breathing.

Who knew she was here? Who had seen her be abducted? Who would look for her, or care? How would she be rescued?

She looked at the chain that ran from her neck collar to the wall. It was far too heavy to break, and—the strangest thing—the door had no knob on the inside: The only way to open it was to insert a key and turn it in the lock. When she had run her hands over the walls, they felt like thick cement. She realized that this bedroom, this cell, had to have been specially constructed in the basement of the house. It was horrifying to think she was trapped in such small quarters.

She had gotten used to her small apartment quickly after leaving home. After all, at home she had spent so much of her time alone in her room anyway. In any case, no matter how small her quarters had been before this, there were windows and the door wasn't locked unless she locked it.

Entrapped, chained, naked, she began to hallucinate. She was sure that since she had arrived and been incarcerated, the room had shrunk a foot on each side. Even the ceiling appeared to have dropped a few inches.

She took deep breaths and swallowed back her tears. Crying, screaming, or pleading did nothing for her. Her kidnappers seemed without compassion, lunatic, on the verge of violent insanity. She had nothing to rely upon but her own innovation, her own thoughts, her own inner strength.

Should she pray? she wondered. Was all this a punishment for what she had done: turned her back on an Orthodox life, turned her back on her father and tradition? Did God really take the time out to judge everyone's actions, no matter how small?

It was silly; this was silly, she told herself. Two crazy people had chosen her. It was just bad luck. Somehow, some way, she would use her creativity and intelligence to extricate herself from this horror. She simply had to get ahold of herself, stop feeling sorry for herself, and start acting like Harry Gold's daughter.

Funny, she thought with a short laugh, how she reverted to that—Harry Gold's daughter—when she wanted to think of herself as strong. Her father was a man of great emotional strength. She knew no one who had his firmness and determination once his mind was made up. Look at how he had dealt with her leaving. He said Kaddish, tore his shirt, and even, according to Miriam, burned a memorial candle on the monthly anniversary of her exodus.

The creaking she heard above became louder until she recognized the sound of footsteps on a stairway. She heard their voices and then, a moment later, heard the door lock being opened. The couple entered, the woman carrying a tray, the man carrying a bottle of water.

"Dinner," the woman sang, and placed the tray

on the maple table. He put the bottle of water beside it. They both turned and smiled at her. "Come on, Anna. You have to eat while everything is still hot."

"I don't want to eat," she said. "I want to go home." Her voice was raspy. Her throat ached from the screaming and crying.

" 'Home is the place where, when you go there, they have to take you in,' " the man recited. "Robert Frost. Anyway, this is your home. We had to take you in," he said.

"This is not my home," Anna retorted, her jaw tight, her lips firm. "You two will be arrested and put in jail for a long time for this."

"Now, that's not very nice," the man said. The woman nodded.

"No, it isn't, Anna."

"What you're doing to me isn't very nice!" Anna shouted back at them. "You're kidnappers!"

The two of them stared at her, both blinking rapidly. Then the man sighed deeply.

"We haven't called you any names, Anna, although we should," he said. "We have every right to treat you like the criminal you are."

"I am not a criminal. You two are the criminals!"

"We had hoped you would cooperate and we could be nice to you," the woman added.

"Of course you're a criminal, Anna," he said. "You were nearly a murderer, you know. You were going to kill an unborn life."

"No I wasn't," Anna cried. "I had only gotten information in case I had to do that. The man who is the father of my child and who I love and who loves me is making plans for us. Now you've taken me away and he won't be able to do what he has to do. He'll think I left him. The baby will be without its father," she said.

"No it won't. I'm the father."

"And I'm the mother," the woman said. "It's like the Immaculate Conception. No one put the seed in me but my baby's coming." She smiled.

Anna tried to swallow, but her throat felt as if it were filled with cork. She closed her eyes and rocked herself.

"We'd like you to eat your dinner," the man said. "It's filled with good things for the baby."

"Daddy's right: You must stay healthy. Remember, you are feeding someone else as well now."

"I won't eat," Anna said defiantly. "I won't drink."

"Hunger strike!" the man shouted.

"Hunger strike!" the woman echoed, screaming it as she might scream fire.

He ran out of the room and the woman charged at Anna, who cringed. The woman seized the chain about six inches from the metal collar and pulled back, choking and forcing Anna to lie back. She coughed, gasped, and pulled on the collar to keep it from her throat while the woman literally dragged her to the headboard, placing a link over a hook that was embedded in the cement wall just above the bed. The effect was to keep Anna back and down.

The man reentered, pushing an IV stand with an IV bag attached. Anna's eyes bulged in disbelief as the woman reached down under the bed and came up with a strap, which she then threw over Anna's chest. The man received it on the other side and buckled it, pinning Anna's arms down. They did the same with a strap at the base of the bed to keep her legs down. With the chain and collar hooked to the wall above her and the straps fastened, she was unable to move or resist.

"Okay, Daddy, she's prepared," the woman said. He rolled the IV over to the bed. Then he took a cotton pad out of his pocket and a bottle of alcohol. He dabbed the cotton pad on the opened bottle and wiped Anna's forearm.

"Just relax," he said. "I won't have any trouble finding a vein. I do this for a living."

"Stop!" Anna screamed. "I'll eat. I promise. I'll eat," she gasped.

The two looked at each other.

"Do you believe her, Mommy?"

"No," she said.

"I swear I'll eat. I promise," Anna begged.

"Maybe I believe her a little bit," the woman relented. "What about you, Daddy?"

"I don't know," he said. He brought the needle

to Anna's arm and held it there. "She's got good veins. This isn't going to be hard, Mommy."

"I worked hard on the dinner, Daddy. If she promises to eat it . . ."

"If you leave one crumb . . ." he said, holding the needle over her face.

"I won't. I promise," Anna said.

"It's getting cold, Daddy," the woman said.

"Okay," he decided. He pulled the IV bag back and went around the bed to unfasten the straps. The woman took the chain off the hook.

Anna sat up slowly, rubbing her arms. The woman took the cover off the dish.

"Meat loaf, potatoes, green beans, and orange Jell-O with real fruit in it for dessert. Of course, we want you to take your vitamin too. Don't we, Daddy?"

"Prenatal vitamins," he said, nodding.

" 'Baby has to be healthy; Baby has to be strong,' " the woman sang, as if it were a nursery rhyme.

Anna got off the bed and went to the table. They stood behind her as she ate. The food nearly choked her, but she forced it down.

"Eat slowly and chew every bite," the woman said.

"Looks good," the man said. "Looks very good."

"We're all going to get along just fine now, aren't we, Daddy?"

"I think we will." He nodded and smiled at Anna. "I have a good feeling about this, Mommy."

Anna closed her eyes and chewed and swallowed. They stood there, watching her, until she finished everything and washed the vitamin down with a glass of water.

"Now, don't you feel better?" the woman asked.

"I feel sick to my stomach," Anna said.

"Natural in your condition, right, Daddy?"

"I've seen it a hundred times, probably two hundred. And you, Mommy, you've seen it twice as many."

"That's for sure. That's for damn sure."

Anna turned and looked at them. Did they work at the clinic? *My God, right-to-lifers working in an abortion clinic?*

"Where do you two work?" she asked.

"That's not important. That's not something you have to know," he replied. "You should ask only questions that are important, questions about your pregnancy," he told her, "so our baby is born beautiful and healthy."

"But how do I know you know what you're talking about?" she said quickly.

"Mommy, how will she know?"

"You'll have to have faith," the woman said. "Do you have any faith? Do you believe in God? Do you pray?"

"I pray," Anna said, nodding at them, her eyes small.

The woman smiled at her coldly.

"If you think you can pray to God to hurt us and

help you, you are praying to the Devil, not to God. God sent us to you. Don't waste His time with silly, evil requests. Pray instead for a healthy baby."

"It's time for her show, Mommy," the man said. He went to the video deck and inserted a tape. Then he turned on the television set.

The set lit up with the title: *Abortion, The Slaughter of the Innocent.*

"You watch this," the woman ordered. "You watch this from beginning to end. We're going to give you a test on it later, and for every question you miss . . ."

"Yes," the man said, "for every question you miss, there'll be some hell to pay."

"Enjoy," the woman said picking up the tray. "Daddy?"

He started to wheel the IV bag out. They both paused at the doorway.

"You're not watching," the woman said, waving her forefinger. "You're going to be very sorry if you don't."

"No," Anna whispered. "*You're* going to be the ones who will be sorry."

Apparently they didn't hear her. They left and closed the door.

On the television screen, bloody, aborted fetuses were displayed.

Anna cringed.

Behind the gruesome pictures a sound track began.

"Rock-a-bye baby in the treetop . . ."

Anna closed her eyes. This was insane. This couldn't be really happening.

"Daddy," she cried. *"Daddy!"* she screamed.

Her voice echoed off the cement walls and died inside her own ears.

8

McShane followed the directions the dispatcher had given him for the only Gold with a residence in Parksville. It took him off Route 17, the highway residents referred to as the Quickway, to a side road called Highland Drive and ran him through some heavily wooded areas with houses far apart from each other until he found the address, a gray two-story Queen Anne–style home set a good five hundred yards in from the road.

The lawn looked in desperate need of cutting. There was a narrow fieldstone walkway from the gravel driveway to the steps of the full-width porch. Weeds grew freely between the stones. To the right and below the porch was a single hardwood bench, the iron legs of which were blotched with patches of rust.

Although the house looked like a fugitive from maintenance, it still appeared to be clean. There

was no litter strewn about; there were no old broken lawn mowers, rusted, broken bikes, or discarded tires and auto parts, as there were in front of so
many tired-looking, dilapidated houses in the eco-
nomically degenerating area. People living in most
of those homes existed on income a notch above
the poverty level. Their pride was as bankrupt as
their pocketbooks. To McShane, many of them
were citizens of a different country: the welfare
state. Indeed, they didn't vote; they had little or
nothing to do with the communities in which they
found themselves subsisting; they sat with vacant
eyes, waiting for some miraculous metamorphosis.

It didn't take much to see how the Catskills had
changed. No longer the vacation mecca it had
been, it was now the target of takeovers by religious groups who pounced on the bankrupt and
near-bankrupt hotels, bungalow colonies, and
rooming houses, turning them into meditational
and Orthodox retreats without the concurrent benefit to area businesses. Like overripe fruits, the
properties fell from the tax rolls, and the mad
downward spiral continued, swallowing up homes
in foreclosures, driving businesses into Chapter 11,
drumming up the unemployment, and swelling the
welfare rolls.

There was a new Chevy station wagon parked in
the Golds' driveway. There was no garage. It was a
little after five o'clock and the sunlight, weakened
by the overcast sky, was nearly gone. McShane

noticed very little illumination in the house and wondered if anyone was home, despite the presence of the station wagon. He pulled in behind it and got out slowly.

Off to the right he could hear the constant liquid sound of car tires as the automobiles whizzed along the Quickway west toward Binghamton, Syracuse, and other northwestern New York locations. The highway turned so it was just beyond the woods to his right. Other than that, it was what he called "country quiet": no horns beeping, no people shouting, no machinery going. There was the occasional call of a bird and the sound of the wind weaving its way through the maples, oaks, and hickory trees. Something might scurry along quickly over the fallen leaves, its small feet tapping and crunching the fallen, dried leaves, but other than that, it was so still that he felt as if he were entering a painting.

McShane wasn't from the Catskills. He had been born in Boston, but his family moved to New York City when his father got a good job with the New York Transit Authority. They lived in Queens, and in those days the only thing he knew about this part of the Catskills was that it was some sort of retreat for middle-class Jewish families who could afford to get their children out of New York during the hot summer months. Once, when he was in his late teens, he rode up here with some friends and they crashed the Concord Hotel, spending a few hours on the grounds, at the pool, and in the nightclub before they were discovered and escorted off by hotel security.

Little did he suspect that, years later, when he left the Army and entered the police academy in New York, he would meet and fall in love with a girl whose family owned a poultry and egg farm in a place called Dairyland, just outside of a hamlet called Woodbourne, all of it barely as big in population as half a New York City block.

Cookie was attending Hunter College then. She was going to become a teacher but evolved into a school psychologist instead, fortuitously just at the time the schools began to need them. She was hired to fill a position in the Fallsburg School District, the school district from which she herself had graduated, and he got a job with the Sullivan County Sheriff's Department and quickly became one of their detectives.

His father-in-law and mother-in-law gave Cookie and him an acre of land and the down payment for the construction of a house as a wedding present. They built a modest three-bedroom ranch-style home and started to talk about having a family, but Cookie, whose real name was Gayle Barbara Lucci, wanted to establish her career and position first. McShane himself was still somewhat terrified of the idea of a baby, and put up little debate.

"Whatever you want, honey," he told her, as if she were talking about nothing more than choosing a new rug for the living room. It was his standard response to almost everything, and she soon began to hold him accountable for his lack of opinion. She said it revealed a deep disinterest in the things they should cherish together. On the other hand, he felt he was damned if he did and damned if he didn't. He accused her of practicing pop psychology on him and their marriage. The strain in the fault line of their marriage began to intensify.

Once he got his promotion to full detective, he became devoted to the position and enmeshed in the work. Missing each other for dinner became more and more the practice and not the exception. But it wasn't just his job that caused him to forget birthdays and other holidays, nor could he blame his work for his often arriving late for family affairs: It seemed it didn't take much to distract him. He would linger in front of a television set to watch a ball game, join some of his buddies for one more beer or a game of pool, and just lose track of time.

His adolescent carefreeness became more and more of a thorn in Cookie's back. She complained, called him Huck Finn, even began keeping a scorecard and pinning it on the kitchen wall.

All of it accumulated until one day she turned on him and read off the bill of complaint.

"If I wanted to be a spinster," she concluded, "I wouldn't have gotten married."

He admitted to the errors and promised to reform, but after a week of reliability, he fell into his old habits. One night she was waiting up for him when he returned from his spontaneously arranged poker game at the firehouse. Before he could begin to apologize, she gave him a choice: *You move out or I move out.*

He pleaded again, making essentially the same promises, and the next day she moved out.

Feeling guilty about that, he moved out too, and she moved back in. Now he either got the answering machine or was told to speak to her attorney.

His mother-in-law and his mother said the same thing: "At least there are no children to suffer through this, as there are with so many couples who break up."

Some compensation, he thought.

He felt like someone who had just stepped off a merry-go-round: He was still spinning and finding it impossible to understand how he got so dizzy. *How did this happen?* he wondered. *How does it happen that you fall in love with someone, want to spend the rest of your life with her, and then mess up the relationship so badly, she can't take the idea of spending one more day in the same house with you? How do you hold someone and tell her how much you love her and do everything intimate two people can do with each other and then become strangers?*

It was a puzzle too hard to solve right now, and anyway, once again, he was being distracted and finding a reason not to deal with the problem.

As he started down the fieldstone walkway toward the front steps, he thought he saw a curtain move in one of the front windows. The steps of the short stairway creaked under his weight, and the floorboards on the porch sounded loose beneath his feet. There was a screen door peppered with small holes. He opened that door first, found no buzzer, and knocked softly with his closed fist. He was greeted with silence, waited, and then knocked again, harder, using his knuckles. A moment later the door was opened by a tall woman who looked to be in her late twenties or early thirties. She had long ebony hair that lay a few inches below her shoulders. She wore a very plain-looking blue-and-white pattern one-piece dress, no jewelry, not even a watch. When she drew closer, he saw she had almond-shaped gray eyes, a dark complexion, and a soft mouth with the lower lip just a bit puffy. Her chin was small and graceful, and her nose was straight but just a trifle pointed.

But it was her eyes that held McShane's attention. It was like looking into the tips of two candles, mesmerizing, warm and yet somehow sad.

"Yes?" she said. He held up his ID. Without a porch light or a light inside the house, he imagined it was difficult if not impossible for her to read.

"My name's McShane. I'm a police detective with the sheriff's department. Is this the home of"—he checked his notepad quickly—"Harry Gold?"

"Yes. What's wrong?" she asked, her voice filling with anxiety.

"Do you have a relative named Anna Gold?"

"She's my . . . she's my sister," she said, and lowered her eyes quickly. "What's wrong?"

"Can I talk to you and your father about her?" he asked.

"What did she do?"

"I'd like to come in and talk about her," he replied.

"Who is it?" a deep voice called from a room behind her.

"It's a policeman, Papa."

"A policeman?"

McShane inched forward as a man in a wheelchair rolled himself into the hallway. A small flicker of illumination cast a yellow glow over his white shirt and graying black beard. Even in a wheelchair, Harry Gold looked formidable. He had shoulders as wide and as thick as McShane's and was obviously close in height. He rolled himself beside his daughter.

"What is it you want?" he asked.

"I've come to talk about an Anna Gold. She's apparently missing, perhaps abducted," McShane blurted. Sometimes, hitting people with the hard news quickly was the best way, he thought, especially when there is some reluctance on their part to speak with you.

The tall woman gasped and brought her closed

right hand to her lips, but Harry Gold barely blinked.

"She was abducted some time ago," he said, nodding.

"What?"

"She was taken almost a year ago."

"I don't understand," McShane said, directing himself more to the woman.

"She left us—left our faith and our ways," she explained.

"Has she called here during the last five or six hours?" he asked.

"She doesn't call here anymore," Harry replied quickly, firmly.

"Well, her car was found open in a supermarket parking lot with her cart of groceries beside it. No one's been able to locate her. She hasn't returned to her apartment, nor has she been taken to the hospital. I'm afraid it looks very suspicious," McShane explained.

The tall, dark-haired young woman gasped.

"I need information," McShane followed.

"It's time for Havdalah," Harry Gold said.

"Pardon?"

"The conclusion of the Sabbath," the tall woman explained.

"Invite him," Harry said, turning his wheelchair.

"Would you like to come in?"

"Sure," McShane said. She stepped back and he entered.

"My name is Miriam," she said, closing the door. He walked beside her as they followed the wheelchair down the corridor to a room on the right in which a large candle with several braided wicks burned in a silver candleholder. It was placed at the center of the dining room table.

"What's this all about?" McShane asked as Harry Gold wheeled himself to the head of the table. She smiled.

"We're ending the Sabbath with this ceremony. During the Sabbath, we do not turn on any lights or burn any candles. This is the Havdalah candle. It symbolizes, as the first act of the new week, the first act of creation which marked the first day of the week when God said, 'Let there be light.' "

"Oh," McShane said, nodding.

"Miriam," Harry said.

"Please, have a seat," she told McShane, and she moved to take the candle from the holder. McShane went to the chair beside her and sat.

"Pour him a glass of wine, Miriam."

"Oh. Yes," she said, and from a silver wine bottle she poured another glass of wine and gave it to McShane.

Harry raised his cup of wine in his right hand. McShane followed suit and watched as Harry Gold recited the prayer.

"For our guest, I will translate," he added. "Blessed art Thou, Lord our God, King of the Universe, who creates the fruit of the vine."

He sipped and so did McShane. Then Harry picked up a small silver box. Harry recited another prayer in Hebrew and translated.

"Blessed art Thou, Lord our God, King of the Universe, who creates diverse spices."

He sniffed it and passed it to Miriam, who sniffed it and passed it to McShane. His eyes widened.

"This is known as a *b'samim* box. It contains sweet spices that we regard as a delight for the soul, rather than for the body. In some small way it makes up for the loss of the additional soul which takes leave at the end of the Sabbath, and for the loss of spiritual strength," she explained.

McShane nodded and sniffed.

Harry then turned back to the candle and recited another blessing, after which he picked up the cup of wine and recited a longer prayer.

After he concluded, Miriam went to the wall switch and turned on the small chandelier.

"Thank you for being patient," Harry Gold said.

"No problem," McShane said. "Kind of interesting too."

Harry smiled and nodded.

"God said, 'A precious jewel have I in My possession, which I wish to give to Israel, and Sabbath is its name.' "

"Yeah, I understand," McShane said quickly.

"Do you?" Harry followed. He smiled again. "Now, that is kind of interesting. My daughter Anna didn't."

McShane nodded.

"It does look like something might have happened to your daughter, Mr. Gold."

"I have no doubt in my mind that something happened to my daughter, Mr. McShane. I have already spent nearly a year in mourning."

"Mourning?"

"She left us—died to us."

"You mean you haven't spoken to her since she left?" McShane asked, looking at Miriam. She lowered her eyes again.

"Not a word," Harry replied. He looked at Miriam. "Isn't that right, Miriam?"

"Yes, Papa," she said, but McShane had an instinctive sense that she was lying.

"So you can't tell me who her friends are, who she might be seeing, if she has any enemies, voiced any fears . . . ?"

"No, nothing," Harry said. "Right after my wife died, Anna became rebellious. She stopped her prayers, refused to follow the kosher laws, neglected the Sabbath, and spent more and more time with people outside of our faith. One day she came to tell me she had gotten a job with the government and would be moving out of our home. We had words and she left."

McShane nodded.

"What is your health problem, if I might ask?"

"I had an operation on my foot last week. It isn't

anything terribly serious. I was in and out in two days, but I have to stay off the foot for six weeks."

"What do you do, Mr. Gold?"

"Now I don't do much. I was a busy mason once. I built many of the walls and fireplaces in the area. My work is well known," he said.

McShane looked at Miriam.

"Miriam keeps my home and waits for the right man to come along," he added.

"Stop, Papa."

"She's shy, but you know what, Mr. McShane? Shy is good. Look at Anna: She was far from shy, and now you've come to tell me something might have happened to her. The day she left, I felt the Angel of Death fly over my house. I saw his shadow behind her."

"Papa!"

"I've said it before," he snapped. "She delivered herself into some evil."

"You have no idea what?"

"Nothing specific," Harry said. His voice was full of bitterness. "Don't criticize me for being angry about it," he added quickly, his eyes fixed on McShane. "Anger keeps me from crying."

McShane nodded and rose.

"Thank you for including me in your Sabbath service," he said. "If I learn anything, I'll call. I'd like to call if I have any questions whose answers might help."

Harry nodded but looked away. McShane turned to Miriam, who quickly shifted her eyes from her father to him.

"I'll see you out, Detective," she said.

"Thank you."

He walked out with Miriam just a step behind him. She flipped on the porch light. At the door he turned.

"You've spoken to her since, haven't you?"

She looked back and stepped out on the porch, closing the door softly behind her. He hadn't noticed it as much before because of the darkness and the shadows, but he thought she was very attractive and, despite the simple, loosely fitted dress, a woman with a full figure. She had a rich, soft complexion, and those gray eyes put a tingle in his blood and made his heart beat just a little faster. He tried not to look obvious about it, and she did indeed seem oblivious to the signals she unintentionally sent and was just as oblivious to his response. He felt an almost childish simplicity about her, an innocence that was as refreshing and surprising as a cold glass of spring water.

"Yes," she whispered. "We've spoken. She told me she had a boyfriend, but he was married. She said he was seriously considering leaving his wife for her. I told her men make false promises sometimes to get what they want."

McShane widened his eyes and Miriam blushed.

"It's something my mother always told me and

something I have read. It's not something I've learned from personal experience."

"You're right. It happens," McShane said.

"Anyway, Anna assured me it wasn't a false promise. She was so certain. I kept asking her, How do you know? What makes you think it will happen? Why are you so sure? She was quiet and then she said . . ."

"What?"

Miriam took a deep breath.

"If my father knew, he would say Kaddish again," she replied.

"Kaddish?"

"The prayer for the dead."

"Knew what?"

"She told me she was pregnant with his child. I was shocked, of course, and then I told her it was wrong to break up someone's marriage that way, and she became angry at me. That was why we haven't spoken since, I think. She knew I wasn't sympathetic."

"Did she give you any names?"

"No, but I thought it was someone she saw often. She seemed to be seeing him every day."

"Pregnant, huh? How pregnant was she?"

"When I spoke last to her, she had just found out. I don't think she was quite two months."

He thought a moment.

"When was the last conversation?"

"Seven, maybe eight days ago. She would call

the house. If my father was home, I would pretend it was the wrong number and then I would go shopping and call her from a pay phone. What do you think has happened to her?"

"I'm not sure yet. I first have to establish she is truly missing."

"Even with her car and groceries left like that in the parking lot?" Miriam asked.

"Yeah, it suggests trouble, of course, but people do strange things. Some guy recently got out of his car in the middle of Main Street in Liberty and walked away, leaving the car running. He just lost it. Maybe all that was happening to her just got to her and she ran off. She ran from here," he added, looking at the house.

Miriam bit down on her lower lip. There were tears in her eyes as she nodded her head gently. He felt like taking her into his arms to comfort her.

"I'm not saying that's definitely it. I've got to get into this more."

She nodded.

He thought again for a moment and then reached into his jacket pocket to take out the button he had found near Anna Gold's car in the supermarket parking lot.

"Does this look familiar?"

Miriam took it and studied it.

"Yes," she said. "I've sewn buttons back on her clothing ever since . . . our mother passed away. This looks like a button on her blue overcoat."

He took it back.

"All right."

"What does that mean?"

"I found it by her car."

"Someone ripped it off?" she asked, her eyes wide with fear.

"I don't know. Could be," he admitted. "It does make it look more like she was forcibly abducted."

"My God, what happened to her?"

"I'm going to do my best to find out," he said. "If you hear from her or remember anything else that might help, call me," McShane added and handed her one of his cards. "I'll call you as soon as I learn anything concrete."

"Thank you." She raised her eyes and they looked at each other quietly for a moment. "Have a good week," she said. He understood it was what was always said at the conclusion of the Sabbath.

"You too."

She nodded and went back into the house, closing the door softly behind her. He stood there a moment and then hurried down the steps and to his car.

Another light went on in the house. Miriam went to a window to close the curtain. He watched her. She paused to look out at him and then the curtain closed.

Her eyes continued to burn in his mind like two Sabbath candles.

What the hell am I doing, sitting here and think-

ing about another woman? he wondered. *I've been separated only a few weeks.*

Or maybe Cookie was right. Maybe they had been separated longer than he had realized.

Life was too complicated for the living, he concluded, and drove off to ponder the things he had learned.

9

The door was unlocked again and the young man who called himself Daddy entered. He wore only a bathrobe and a pair of slippers himself. His hair was wet, suggesting he had just come from a shower. He glanced at the television set, which was now a screen of snow, the audio just static since the tape had ended. Then he looked at Anna and smiled because she was sitting on the bed, staring at the set as if something were still being played.

He didn't realize it, but like a small, terrified animal, Anna had burrowed deeply within herself and had shrunken into a tiny, tight ball. Her body had become merely a shell, so that her eyes no longer saw, her ears no longer heard. She had anesthetized herself to shut off the pain.

The young man stared at her a moment longer and then turned off the television set.

Anna blinked but said nothing.

"I don't think you're ready to take the test yet, are you, Anna?" he asked her.

She blinked, but said nothing.

The young man shook his head.

"Mommy sent me down with it," he said, waving a paper. Anna stared blankly and made no response. He shook his head. "She's not going to like this. She has no patience for this sort of behavior, Anna. Mommy thinks you're being cooperative. I would hate to go up and tell her you weren't. Anna?"

Anna blinked a bit faster but said nothing.

He approached her and looked into her face as if he were looking through a small window at the outside world. Then he went to the door and locked it. He stood there a moment.

"I'll help you answer the questions this time, Anna, but I won't next time," he warned in a loud whisper. "If Mommy knew I was helping you, she would be madder at me than she would be at you, and one thing I can't stand is Mommy being mad at me."

He put the paper on her lap. When he smoothed it out, the palm of his hand lingered between her legs. Her blinking increased. He smiled and produced a pen. Tilting his head to read, he recited the first question.

"Number one, once the egg is fertilized with the sperm, how long does it take before the egg begins to divide into cells and embeds itself in the wall of the uterus?" He paused and waited. Then he smiled as if he had heard her reply. "That's right, Anna. Good," he said, and made a mark on the paper. He tilted his head and read again.

"At this early stage of development, what is the growing organism called?" He waited. "What? Right. An embryo. Good, Anna." He made another mark.

His questions and answers continued this way until he reached "How does the mother's body begin to change during the first trimester?" He paused, smiled, and brought his face very close to hers. "You don't have to think too hard about this one, Anna, do you?"

His hands moved to her breasts.

"Don't your breasts feel fuller? Don't they tingle? Of course, I don't know how large your breasts were before, do I, Anna? How large were they? Or is it too early to tell the difference? I don't really know that much about maternity. Mommy's the mommy expert. But," he added, his hands still gliding over her breasts and along her ribs, "your body is a wonderful place for a baby to be formed. That's not true for every woman either. I've seen women who look like they would be the last place I would want my baby formed."

His fingers paused at her nipples. He rolled his thumbs over them, tracing them beneath the soft nightie. His breathing quickened, his eyes grew smaller.

"Baby's lips are going to like this. Yes, they will."

Small beads of sweat broke out on his brow. His tongue glided over his lips.

"Mommy understands that I have to feel like Daddy, you know. She understood before; she'll understand now," he said.

He took the test paper from her lap and put it on the table. Then he stared at Anna a moment before he said almost in a whisper, "I'm sure you can understand too."

Anna didn't turn her head; Anna didn't hear him. She didn't see him drop his robe to his feet, and she didn't feel his hand on her shoulder. There was just a little resistance to the pressure he put on her upper body before she was forced back. Her head was on the pillow, her eyes fixed on the ceiling. She blinked, her eyelids closing for a full second before she opened them, only to blink the same way once again.

She didn't feel his hands move the nightgown up her legs and over her hips. He grunted and crawled over her and between her thighs.

"Got to feel like Daddy," he chanted. "Got to make a baby too."

When he entered her, she started to scream, but her mouth locked open and her tongue lay still. The scream began and died somewhere deep within her where she was closed up in the fetal position, a fist, squeezing harder, tighter.

She couldn't hear his grunts and his chants.

"It's just Daddy," he said. "It's just Daddy making a baby. Don't be afraid."

He shuddered as if he had a cold chill down his spine and grew still, but there was just the slightest realization in Anna that he had finished and withdrew. He lifted himself and sat back, gazing at her glassy eyes, her mouth still agape, and then he looked frantically at the door.

He got off the bed quickly and put on his robe.

"You better stop this, Anna. If Mommy sees you this way, she'll . . . change her mind about you. She'll think you won't be a good baby-maker and then . . . then you'll have to be disposed of, Anna."

Anna didn't move. He returned to the bed and pulled her nightie down. He tucked her under the cover and patted the pillow before placing it beneath her head. Her head felt like a melon in his hands. He couldn't stand looking at that open mouth and tried to close it, but her jaw was locked.

"Stop this, Anna. Stop this now." He raised his hand as if to slap her, but she didn't react and he lowered it.

"You'll be all right," he decided. "You'll have a good night's rest and you'll be fine." He picked up the test paper. "Mommy will be so happy when she sees your answers on the test," he said, and stroked her hair tenderly. "It's very important you understand the miracle happening inside you."

Then he smiled.

"I'm going to be a father. I'll be a good father

too," he added. "Don't you worry about that. Don't you worry about anything. You just go to sleep and dream good dreams. Dream of the baby going, 'Goo-goo.' That's what Mommy dreams of every night. She tells me. The baby's going, 'Goo-goo,' and in her dream she's feeding the baby at her breast and she looks absolutely radiant. Just dream that," he advised.

He took a deep breath, gazed around like a proud father, and strutted to the door. "Good night. Mommy will see you in the morning, and I'll see you after work.

"It's wonderful, how we all just get along, isn't it?" he added.

He unlocked the door, flipped off the lights, stepped out, and closed the door. After he locked it, he walked away, his footsteps quickly growing softer and softer on the stairway until they were gone.

Anna blinked, even in the darkness.

Some moments later she began to unfold herself within and gradually grow until she fit her body again. She was positive that she had just regained consciousness and everything that had happened to her, right up to the last hour, was nothing more than a nightmare.

Thank God, she thought, *thank God, I'm only dreaming.* She breathed relief and then sat up quickly, but the chain rattled and the collar fell against her throat. It was as if someone had poured a glass of ice water down the back of her neck to assure her that she was in reality.

She moaned and crawled off the bed. It was so dark. She started to whimper, when suddenly the door was thrust open. She hadn't even heard the lock being turned or any footsteps on the stairway.

He was there again. He appeared as if he had never truly left but instead had lingered on the other side of the door.

He flipped on the light. Anna shut her eyes.

"I'm so sorry," he said. "I completely forgot to put on the night-light in the bathroom for you. Mommy reminded me and sent me back and, sure enough, here you are, struggling to find your way, aren't you? Mommy is so smart. She just knows everything that's going to happen before it does. Anyway, I'm glad you're feeling better."

He crossed the room, went into the bathroom, and turned on a small light.

"There you are," he said. "Happy dreams."

He flipped off the ceiling light, closed and locked the door again, and walked away. She heard him move quickly up the stairway.

Anna looked toward the bathroom. She felt so tired, even too tired to walk the few yards, but she did so.

Afterward she returned to the bed and fell on her side, folding her legs in the fetal position and putting her hand to her mouth. She lay there for a while, just listening to her heart pound and that

monotonous grinding noise coming from beyond
the walls.

He raped me, she thought. *Oh, God, he raped
me.* She felt contaminated and wanted to tear the
skin off her body. How many ways and how many
times would she be violated? Pity for herself quickly changed to rage.

"They can't do this to me," she muttered. The
defiance built in her and she pumped up her
courage. "I won't let them do this."

She rose and followed the chain back to where
it was embedded in the wall. She pulled until it cut
into the palms of her hands, but she didn't budge
it an iota from where it was attached.

Even if she could open that door, she thought,
she couldn't escape until she found a way to break
this chain. All they had left her was a toothbrush,
a hairbrush, soap, shampoo, toilet paper. She
didn't know if there was anything else in the room.
She went to the light switch and turned it on. Then
she returned to where the chain was embedded
and studied the hook that had been screwed into
the cement wall. The chain was attached to that.
She tried to turn the hook, but she didn't have the
strength.

There must be a way, she thought. *There must be.*
She walked around the small room, looking for
something to use as a tool. She was the daughter
of a stonemason; she had watched her father work
for years. Something of his mechanical talent must

have been passed through to her in the genes. She paused in the bathroom doorway and considered the plumbing. Her gaze centered on the bathtub faucet handles. She studied them a moment. They were long, narrow, and looked like they were made of stainless steel. She turned one in the opposite direction and, as she had hoped, it unscrewed.

Once it was off, she took it back to the hook in the wall, put it through the eye to use it the way she had seen her father use a crowbar, and tried to turn the screw. It didn't budge. She paused, took a deep breath, and tried again, pulling the bottom of the faucet with two fingers of her left hand as she pushed on the top with her right. There was a tiny movement.

Encouraged, she put all her strength behind another attempt, pressing her body weight into it. Again there was just a tiny movement. She paused, caught her breath, and then, using the base of her palm like a hammer, struck the faucet handle repeatedly. It reddened her palm and hurt, but she kept it up. Some of the cement flaked away and the screw turned just a bit more.

She paused again, regained her strength, and tried to turn, laying her entire body weight against the top of the handle. She discerned more of a movement. She had caused almost a quarter of a turn. Heartened, she kept it up until she was exhausted.

But now at least she had hope. She could eventually free this chain from the wall and thus make it possible to walk out of here, even with the chain attached to the collar around her neck. But first, of course, she had to get that door open, or hope that they would forget to lock it once.

She gazed at the faucet handle. It was scratched and even a bit dented from her use of it as a tool. They might notice that, she thought. She quickly wiped up the tiny particles of cement that had been chipped away and then returned the faucet handle to its place on the tub.

She would just have to be alert and wait for an opportunity, but she wouldn't die here and she would never let these two horrible people have the baby growing inside her.

Hope stopped her tears, silenced her screams, and gave her the strength to go to sleep, even in this prison of madness.

10

At the first traffic light, McShane dug into his pocket and produced the index card with Lidia Ambrook's address. She was the one who had left a message on Anna Gold's answering machine. Her address took him past the Monticello trotter racetrack to a complex of modest cream stucco town houses. He located Lidia's unit and pulled into the closest parking space.

The chill that he had felt earlier intensified after the sun had dropped under the horizon. A shelf of Arctic air was clearing the way for winter, leaving no doubt that the first snowfall was imminent. The last two winters had been characterized more by sleet than snow. Icy rains filled with pneumonia and flu fell from the angry skies. Now, with his separation and divorce from Cookie looking more and more inevitable, McShane toyed with the idea of migrating to a warmer climate, maybe the

Southwest. Of course, everyone would accuse him of running from his problems instead of solving them, which was Cookie's chief accusation. But he could live with that, couldn't he? Especially while he basked in the warm sunshine and lounged with a tumbler full of gin and tonic. He might find some soft security-guard or patrolman position, maybe work for one of those private surveillance companies that cruised through private communities, reassuring the wealthy residents. Their biggest problem was probably teenage vandals.

The question—and he recognized it as a legitimate question—was: Was he ready for the slow death? He would grow soft, complacent, years before his time.

"Your problem is simple to diagnose," Cookie told him after she calmed down following a recent blowup. "You're afraid of personal responsibility, Jimmy. You're an adolescent in an adult's body. I'm tired of waiting for you to grow up."

"Really?" he said, his face crimson.

"Yes, really. You're out there playing cops and robbers with all your toys, and when you come home, you're bored. Think about it: You're always trying to find something to distract you, something that will help postpone a decision. If it's not the job, it's football or baseball or your card game with your buddies. You're relieved every time I make a decision for us."

She put her hands on her hips and fired on, her

blue eyes blazing. "Do you know what our mortgage is, Jimmy? Do you know how much we pay for home owner's insurance? How much do we spend on electric, gas, and water every month?"

"You're good at all that, so I let you do it."

"You *let* me!" She laughed. "You think I *want* to do it? Jesus, Jimmy."

"If you're so smart and you know all this about me, why did you marry me in the first place?" he demanded.

"How come you're such a good detective when it comes to everyone and everything else but your own life?" she shot back.

"Just answer the questions, Cookie. Why did you marry me if I'm such a fuckup, huh?"

"Because you're good at what you do, Jimmy. You went undercover and pretended to be a grown-up. You had me fooled," she replied.

He felt as if the top of his head would split open. There was a surge of blood up his veins and into his neck. He couldn't swallow. She saw how angry he was and turned away. He fumed for a moment and then took a deep breath and walked out. Somewhere along the line they definitely had lost it, and maybe it was his fault, or maybe— maybe—she had just outgrown him. The reason didn't seem to matter as much, and that, he at least recognized, was the first sign of the inevitable end.

It could be, he thought—it could be—he was still an adolescent. Cookie wasn't the first to characterize him that way. His brother Robert loved to point out that he got along better with Robert's teenage son than he did with Robert: They had more in common. Robert was an accountant living in Yonkers. He had a son and a daughter and had been married nearly sixteen years. There were only four years separating him and Robert, but it was as if one of them had been adopted. Robert was studious, always well organized, neat, actually meticulous, and the one their mother turned to whenever there was a problem. Robert had always been the responsible one.

"Maybe," Cookie had concluded the last time they had a civil conversation, "your problem is you just don't believe in anything, Jimmy. I'm not saying you have to be religious, but you have to find something bigger than yourself—bigger than your own immediate comfort and pleasure. I know you don't believe in the justice system, even though you risk your life bringing in criminals. You don't think of yourself as especially important either, do you? If you don't do it, someone else will come along and do it, right? And it's not that you're doing something for society; you're just doing it because it's something you can do, something you think you enjoy and something that brings in a paycheck.

"You have no passion for anything, Jimmy. It's no wonder you have no passion for our marriage either," she said, shaking her head and leaving.

All of these conversations and confrontations

were haunting him these days. They hovered around him like buzzards waiting for an opportunity to peck on his dead brain. He hated the quiet moments for that reason, and for that reason it was better to keep busy, go, go, go, until he was ready to pass out every night.

He approached Lidia Ambrook's unit and pressed the buzzer. There was a blue and white welcome mat in front of the door and he could see dainty light-blue curtains in the windows. He waited and then pressed the buzzer again. It was after seven, he thought. She might have gone to dinner. Christ, he himself had forgotten to eat. He wondered why he still wasn't very hungry.

The door opened and a young woman about five feet seven with a rather plain face and dull, short red hair greeted him with a look of hesitation and some fear. In her right hand she held a Taser, which he knew was capable of jamming his nervous system and instantly incapacitating him for up to fifteen minutes.

"Evening," he said quickly, and produced his ID and badge. "I'm investigating the disappearance of a friend of yours."

"Disappearance?"

"Anna Gold."

"Anna's disappeared?"

He quickly told her what had been found in the Van's Supermarket lot, and she lowered the Taser to her side.

"That's horrible. I was wondering why I hadn't heard from her."

"You left a message on her machine. That's how I found you," McShane said. "May I come in?"

"Oh. Yes. I'm sorry," she said stepping back. "I was getting ready to go out."

"I won't take up much time," he said. "I see you're a careful woman," he said, nodding at the Taser.

"Yes," she said. "Someone was attacked here recently. She was nearly raped in the parking lot."

"Really? I didn't know that."

"What do you think's happened to Anna?" she asked, leading him to a small living room.

"I don't have much to go on yet. How long have you two been friends?"

"A few months. I work for the county clerk and Anna works for the public defender, so we met at the government building and started to go out together occasionally. Then she got involved with someone and we haven't been doing all that much together socially."

Lidia lowered herself to the blue-and-white-pattern sofa, the Taser still clutched in her hand like a club. McShane gazed around. With the blue curtains, the light-blue rug, and some of the other pieces of furniture in a matching sapphire shade, it was obvious what was her favorite color. She was even wearing an aquamarine pantsuit. Not that the color made any difference in her case, he thought.

"I just knew something was going to happen to her. I just knew it," she muttered, shaking her head.

"Why?"

"Her astrological chart. I'm into that," she said. "I told her this was a bad month for change. We're both Pisces," she added, her eyes wide.

McShane swallowed a smirk and flipped open his notepad. This was promising to be a waste of his time.

"Do you know the man with whom she had become involved?"

"No," she said. She said it so quickly, he looked up.

"Oh?"

"She wanted to keep it secret. You see, he's a married man. But she said it would soon be known because he was going to get a divorce and leave his wife for her. That's when I read her chart and told her about it being a bad month for change, especially romantic changes."

"When was the last time you saw her?"

"Friday, after work. Frankly, I thought she was going to be very disappointed and there really wouldn't be any dramatic change in her life. But she wouldn't listen, even though I pointed it out logically," she added.

"How did you do that?"

"I could tell from just the way this clandestine romance was being conducted. She said she couldn't call him either at home or at work. She told me she always had to wait for him to call her, and they met in the most out-of-the-way places, traveling great distances for a tryst. It's exactly like what happened in *Love on the Run.*"

"Pardon?"

"*Love on the Run,* a Grace Blush romance novel. It was on the best-seller list for months this year. Eventually the heroine realizes she's being used and abused and exposes her phony lover for what he is."

"I missed that one," McShane said.

"Just like the heroine in the book, she would think nothing of driving fifty miles to have a rendezvous. It was usually an expensive restaurant or an expensive motel. No fleabags. Anna made a point of telling me all that. She thought the more he spent on her, the more committed he was. She bought everything he said hook, line, and sinker. She would go anywhere to meet him. Once she even went to New York City to meet him. I pointed out how the man in *Love on the Run* did the same thing, but she just ignored me."

She sighed and shook her head.

"I gave her the best advice I could."

"This isn't a chapter in a romance novel. It's very serious, so whatever you know, you should tell me," he said.

She stared at him as if deciding whether or not to say something more.

"Why is it so important to know who she was seeing?"

"I've got to follow up on any lead," he explained. "I've already seen her family."

"I bet they weren't any help. You probably know her father and she didn't get along." She shook her head. " 'Didn't get along'—that's an understatement. He's very religious. Kept her chained in on Friday night and Saturday. She wanted to be on her own and have her own life and make her own choices. That's the price you pay sometimes. My mother doesn't always approve of the things I do either, but she's a different generation. We can't be like our parents; we have to be ourselves." She paused and shook her head. "This is terrible. This is so terrible!"

"Is there anyone you can think of who might want to do her harm?"

"No," she said, shaking her head slowly. "She never said anything about anyone like that. As far as I knew, the only one to be angry at her was her own father." Her eyes grew big. "Do you think he might have something to do with it?"

"I have no reason to think that, no."

"He was so angry at her, she couldn't call home. He did something Jewish people do when someone dies, rip his shirt or light some candle. I don't remember exactly. She knew that he was doing it every month and it made her very sad. I don't have any Jewish friends, really, and none that are religious, so I don't know much about it."

"Uh-huh. Did you ever meet anyone when you

went out who might have had some interest in Anna?"

"I don't know why I went out with her," she said instead of answering his question. "All she talked about was . . . this clandestine love of her life. She wasn't interested in any of the guys we saw at the dance clubs. They were all either too immature or . . . not good-looking enough for her."

Her eyes brightened and her face took on the tinge of indignation.

"It's hard, you know, when you go out with someone and you can have someone interested in you but your girlfriend isn't interested in meeting anyone. Everyone goes out in pairs these days. It's safer, but for me, going out with Anna was usually a waste of time."

"So why did you call her to go out with her tonight?"

"All my other friends were busy," she replied.

McShane nodded but thought to himself that she was fantasizing.

"Did she tell you anything else about herself—anything personal?"

"What do you mean?"

"I'm just looking for clues," he replied. He was really looking to see if Anna Gold had mentioned her pregnancy. He couldn't see Lidia leaving it out, but he wanted to be sure.

She thought a moment.

"Nothing. Only what her chart told me. It was the wrong time for change. I warned her: Anything new in her life right now, anything different, could be dangerous." She shook her head and then gazed up at him quickly. "What's your birthday?"

"October twenty-sixth."

"Scorpio. My brother's sign too." Her face turned a bit grayer and she shook her head sadly.

"What's up for me?"

"Stay away from anything involving finances this month," she warned. "Something will happen to change your economic condition, and not for the better."

"No problem," he said. He was about to make a joke when he remembered his divorce. "Maybe you oughta do charts on horses and predict winners."

He handed her one of his cards.

"If you think of anything specific that might help me, please call."

"Okay."

He paused at the door.

"Thanks." He smiled. "At least you should have better luck tonight," he said.

"Pardon?"

"You're going out alone, aren't you?"

"Oh." She shook her head. "I'm just meeting my mother for dinner," she said. "I don't like going out alone. As I told you, I don't feel safe." Her eyes widened. "And now, after you've told me about Anna, even more so!"

McShane nodded and started out.

It really was hard for a young, single woman today, especially if she happened to be as unsophisticated as Anna Gold appeared to have been.

What was it going to be like for Cookie? he wondered, and for the first time, as if it were an idea completely out of the blue, he wondered if she already had someone else.

Maybe she was right about something else: Maybe he was a terrible detective when it came to his own life.

11

You were right, Mommy," he said when he returned to their bedroom. "When I opened the door, I found her grappling with the darkness. I don't know how I forgot to put on the bathroom light for her."

"I know how. You're just excited," she said. Her thin metal-framed reading glasses rested on the bridge of her nose. She was sitting up in bed reading Dr. Spock. She had read *Dr. Spock's Baby and Child Care* at least five times before, and she had underlined many passages.

"Yes, I *am* excited," he agreed, a wide smile on his face. "This time it's really going to happen, isn't it?"

"If you're careful and you do what I tell you, and . . . if you don't forget to do things like put on the bathroom light," she warned.

He laughed and took off his robe. Then he

crawled under the blanket and snuggled up against her.

"It's colder tonight, isn't it?" he asked.

She looked at him askance, suspicious of his motive.

"No, I mean it. It feels like winter's knocking on the door."

"Don't answer it," she said, and he laughed. "What are you working tomorrow, the eight-to-four shift?"

"Eight to four and then I'll hurry home."

"Call first. We'll always need something, now that the baby's on the way."

"I will. Boy, am I tired," he said and yawned. "It's been a long day, hasn't it?"

She continued to read. He closed his eyes, and then the phone rang. His eyes snapped open. It rang again. Her eyes went to the clock.

"He's right on time. I'll talk to him," she said. She closed the book and set it on her lap before reaching for the receiver. "Hello?" She looked at him as she listened. He stared at the ceiling. "It went fine," she said, "just as we promised it would. No, she's resting comfortably by now. She ate a good dinner too. . . . No. I told you, we were very careful. . . . I know, and we're grateful. Thank you."

She listened. He turned because she was listening so long without speaking, but she was nodding her head as if the speaker could see her.

"I understand. . . . I don't see any reason why we

would have to call you, anyway. . . . Yes. . . . Good-bye, and good luck to you too."

She replaced the receiver carefully and sat back with a deep sigh.

"So?"

"Everything's fine. He's satisfied with us."

"What did you mean when you said you didn't see any reason for us to call him anyway?"

"He asked that we don't call and never come by."

"Oh. Right, right."

They looked at each other, both so excited and happy that they couldn't stop smiling. Suddenly she got out of the bed.

"Where are you going?"

"I can't help it. I've got to look one more time before I go to sleep."

"But it will all be there in the morning, silly."

"I know. I just can't help it, and it helps me fall asleep. It fills my head with good dreams," she replied firmly. "Stop being so critical."

He shook his head as she hurried out of the bedroom. After a moment he rose and, naked, followed. She was standing in the nursery bedroom doorway, looking in at everything. He stepped up beside her and took her hand. Without speaking, they both gazed at the bassinet, the baby basin, the rattles, and the pile of real cloth diapers on the changing table. She didn't mind washing them. Modern-day mothers with their disposable diapers weren't as committed to their babies as they should be, she believed.

She let go of his hand and walked to the dresser. She opened the top drawer and reached in for a baby's sleeping outfit. This one was blue, for a boy, but the one beside it in the drawer was pink, for a girl.

"Which do you think it will be?" he asked when she held up both of them.

She thought a moment.

"It just feels like a girl," she said. "A precious little dainty princess." She put the blue one back and cradled the pink one in her arms as if there were a baby in it.

"Who you will spoil terribly," he said.

"So what?" she snapped back at him. "No one spoiled *me*. My older sister, Tami, she was spoiled, and so was my brother, Teddy, but my mother was tired and I was an accident. She never stopped reminding me about that whenever I did something wrong."

"I know," he said. He did. He had heard the story many times before.

"If I spilled something at the table or broke something, she would slap me and say, 'None of this should be. You shouldn't even be here.' "

He shook his head.

"Your mother didn't know how lucky she was, having a healthy child. She should have thanked her stars."

"She didn't thank anyone or anything and especially not my father. He would look at me and say, 'Thanks to you, she won't let me live.' "

She returned the outfit to the drawer and closed it.

"Let's go back to bed," he said. "We've got big days ahead of us and we'll need our strength."

She nodded and, with her head down, followed him to their bedroom. After they were under the blanket again, she bit her lower lip and choked back a sob.

"What?" he said.

"When I was looking at you standing there in the doorway with your pendulum dangling like the pendulum in the grandfather's clock, I thought how you must hate me for being sterile."

"That's ridiculous, Mommy, and you know it. I couldn't ever hate you for any reason."

"But you're armed for bear and I'm . . . I'm an empty woods."

He laughed.

"It's not funny."

"I'm not laughing at you; I'm laughing at what you said: 'armed for bear.' "

"Well, you are, aren't you? Don't you tell me how you're so full to the brim, you just explode at the most unexpected times? Even driving to work?"

"I'm sorry I told you that, Mommy."

"No you're not."

"I am," he insisted. "I shouldn't tell you things that might make you feel bad."

"We promised never to lie to each other and never to keep secrets, ever. We agreed, Daddy."

"I know, but now you're making me feel sorry for telling you."

"I'm sorry if I did that, but I just felt . . ."

"Don't say it," he warned.

She bit down on her lower lip and her cheeks bloated as if the words she kept in were inflating and putting pressure on her mouth. Finally, she released it in a puff of air, too inarticulate to be understood.

They were both quiet. She put the book on the night table and turned off the light. Their eyes remained open in the darkness, however. They both lay there, listening. They had lain there before like that, and they knew the sounds of the house and the sounds that should be coming from below. They were so used to the monotonous grinding noise from outside, they didn't hear it anymore. But they heard the wood walls and floors creak, and heard the wind become fingers scratching at the windows. Suddenly she heard what sounded like a muffled scream.

"What was that?" she asked.

He listened. "I didn't hear anything."

"I did." After a pause she added, "Maybe she's doing something to herself; maybe she's doing something to our baby."

"Now, don't get crazy, Mommy."

She sat up with such force, the bed shook. And then she spun around and put her fingers around his eyeballs, her nails sharp and long and pressing just enough to convince him that, in a split second, she could tear his eyes out.

"Don't ever call me crazy," she said, her words escaping her lips like air leaking from a tire. "I told you that a thousand times if I told you once."

"I'm sorry, Mommy. I didn't mean *crazy*. I meant, don't get upset."

Her fingers relaxed and he let out his own breath.

"I've got to be sure I didn't hear anything bad," she said, and got out of the bed. She opened the night table drawer and took out the flashlight.

"Mommy," he pleaded.

"No. You remember the last time. You remember what she did to herself . . . all the blood and then our baby," she wailed. "I want this baby, Daddy. I want this baby. It's going to be a girl. I'm sure."

"Mommy," he said, but she was already out the door.

He rose like an arthritic old man to go after her. He heard her open the basement door and then go quietly down the stairs without putting on the light. She just used the flashlight. He knew why. He stood at the top of the steps and listened. She was tiptoeing across the basement floor to the maternity room. She took the key off the rack so quietly, only he would know it, and then she inserted it sharply into the lock, turned it, and thrust open the door.

Anna raised her hands instinctively as the beam of the flashlight hit her face. She couldn't see the woman until she was at the foot of the bed. She realized the woman was standing there naked.

Anna's heart pounded. She cringed as the woman reached down and drew back the blanket, directing the beam at Anna's legs and stomach. Then she leaned over Anna, pulling her nightie up her legs. Anna screamed, but she ignored her as she inspected.

"What do you want? Please. Let me go. Please."

The woman brought her face closer. Her taut, small breasts were white as bone, and her shoulders glistened like alabaster in the wake of the flashlight's glow. Her eyes appeared luminous, two glittering dimes. She drew closer until her face was only inches from Anna's.

"Don't you hurt my baby," she said through her teeth. "Don't you do anything to hurt her."

Anna whimpered and pressed her palms over her breasts. She was back as far as she could go.

"If I hear my baby scream again, I'll make you very sorry," she threatened. "Do you understand? Do you?"

"Yes," Anna said, nodding.

"Good." She retreated. "Good." She took a deep breath and then walked to the doorway. In the dim glow of the bathroom light, the woman's backbone appeared embossed. She was very thin, her shoulder blades distinct, sharp. It was like watching a skeleton for a moment, and that put another chill into Anna's heart. She could barely breathe.

The woman turned in the doorway.

"Good night," she said softly, sweetly. Then she walked out and closed the door. Anna heard the lock snapped shut.

He still waited on the stairway.

"Mommy?" he said as she approached.

"It's all right. Everything's fine," she said.

"Good. Let's go to sleep, Mommy. I've got to be up bright and early and fresh for work. You wouldn't want me making mistakes with people's veins, would you?"

"No," she agreed as she came up the stairway. He waited until she was almost there and then he returned to the bedroom. She came in and put the flashlight back in the night table drawer. Then she crawled under the covers beside him.

"I'm so tired," she said.

"Me too."

"It was a long day, wasn't it?"

"Very long."

"But a good day. The best day."

"The best," he agreed.

"We did good, Daddy. He told me on the phone. He said, 'You guys did real good.' "

Daddy laughed.

They were both quiet for a moment and then, low—so low, she didn't hear him for a moment—Daddy began to sing.

"Ninety-nine baby bottles of milk on the wall, ninety-nine baby bottles of milk. If one of the bottles should happen to fall . . ."

"Ninety-eight baby bottles of milk on the wall."

They laughed and hugged each other. He kissed her cheeks and her forehead and then her lips. She kissed his eyes, the eyes she had nearly ripped out.

"Sweet dreams," he said.

"Sweet dreams."

She giggled. He laughed and cuddled against her.

The fingers of the wind moved over the roof and then moved on into the darkness and down the long road of night toward the promise of another day. They were both positive that every day would be better than the day that had come before it. And, after all, that was the meaning of true happiness and contentment.

12

Despite the lateness of the hour, the commotion around the county lockup seemed even more intense. A half-dozen television station trucks with their satellite dishes atop were in the parking lot. Clumps of radio and print reporters were gathered around the main entrance, many of them still quite animated. Some of the patrolmen had been pulled in from their regular highway beats to assist and were speaking near the reporters, looking almost as excited themselves.

McShane parked and sauntered toward the entrance. Anyone new on the scene attracted everyone's attention. He could see people asking the patrolmen if they knew who he was. Leo Hallmark, a tall, light-brown-haired twenty-two-year-old, stepped forward to greet him. They often played racquetball at the gym, and it was important for McShane's ego to beat him whenever he could.

"Where the hell you been, McShane? Everyone else's been chained to the fort."

"I knew you guys would have it all under control," Jimmy said. "What's been happening?"

"He confessed. It was wild. No remorse."

"Who confessed?"

"The leader, someone named Roy Gault. He claims he obeyed a higher moral law and can't be held accountable for killing the doctor who kills babies. He doesn't recognize the authority of our police and justice system, which he says is run by the Devil. So, welcome to hell."

"It's like a disease," McShane said, shaking his head. "You sit in your living room and watch it on television happening far away, thinking it's someone else's problem, and then, before you know it, it starts to spread and—"

"It's in your own backyard. Seriously, where you been? Even the janitors are on overtime."

"Investigating a missing person, a young woman who appears to have been abducted in the Van's Supermarket parking lot early this afternoon."

"No shit? In broad daylight?"

"Would I kid you? How's the sheriff?"

"Not in a good mood. You know how he gets when he doesn't have a nap."

McShane laughed.

"I know how I get."

"We still on for Tuesday morning?"

"Far as I know. Prepare to lose again."

"We'll see."

McShane continued into the station. Ralph Cutler came down the corridor from the holding cells, lumbering as if his upper body were just along for the ride. His big head actually wagged with each plodding step. He glared at McShane and then gestured with his eyes toward his office. McShane followed. At the doorway Cutler turned.

"They want to know why it took us so long to get a patrol car to the clinic. They cut me back five personnel from last year. I've got thousands of square miles to cover, and the chairman of the county board of supervisors wants to know why we didn't get there before the state police."

"Didn't the clinic call the state police first?"

The sheriff nodded and raised his hands.

"You're going to go and apply some logic to this?"

He entered his office. McShane followed and took a seat while the sheriff made a phone call to his wife.

"I don't know when I'll be home tonight, if at all," he told her. "I did take my pill. . . . I know, I know . . ." he said, rolling his eyes at McShane. "Don't be waiting on me, Lois. . . . I'm not still here because I want to be. In fact, this is the last place I want to be. I'd even go to dinner at your sister's."

Whatever his wife replied made him smirk. He said good-bye, put the phone back on its cradle, and sat back.

"It was a madhouse," he said. "You missed the best of it: State dicks are racing around with the print results, and all of a sudden this Roy Gault steps forward and admits he heaved his cross at the doctor. Turns out, the thing is more like a boomerang. I mean, it's deliberately made to be a weapon. When we asked him how he could do that with such an important religious symbol, he says, What better weapon than the cross to end the murder of innocent children? These people are beyond control." He took a deep breath and held his hand against his diaphragm as though he were having heartburn.

"You all right?"

"Yeah, yeah. I got reporters having orgasms, lawyers coming out of the walls screaming at the DA's people that their clients had a right to protest and can't be charged with accessory to murder, cameras everywhere, and politicians ringing the phone off the hook, wanting to know why we didn't see this coming. How, they want to know, could fifty people drive down one of our county's highways, surround a clinic, start a demonstration, and the sheriff not know about it? And in broad daylight!"

McShane nodded sympathetically. He knew his boss well by now. It was better to remain silent at this stage, let him vent, and look sympathetic rather than offer any comment, which would more than likely be misunderstood.

"Forget the fact that we're investigating traffic accidents, enforcing speed limits, assisting in fires, transporting prisoners. . . . I'm stretched so thin, I could be made into shoelaces.

"I have to meet with these government people at nine and update them on my internal investigation tomorrow. On Sunday I'm supposed to run an internal investigation of our response time while all this is going on," he wailed.

McShane shook his head. Ralph Cutler stared at him a moment as if he had forgotten who he was. Then he sat forward, took another deep breath, and relaxed.

"So what do you have?"

"I'm afraid it's definitely breaking out like some sort of abduction. I visited with the family. The woman was estranged from her father. There's no mother. Just an older sister," he added. "Sister's been in contact with her, but not the father. Treats her as if she's dead."

"Dead?"

"They're religious Jews. Apparently she turned her back on their ways, whatever, and he feels she betrayed the faith."

"What happened to this country?" the sheriff asked, arms out. "Everything's wrapped around religious beliefs. Everyone's got a direct line to the

Almighty and feels he or she can do anything they
want because God told them to do it."

His eyes widened.

"Maybe that's what I should tell the board of
supervisors tomorrow," he quipped. "I do only
what God tells me to do."

"Yeah, well, I got the missing woman's address
and phone number from her checkbook and went
to the apartment."

"What's her name?"

"Anna Gold, twenty-six, works for the public
defender's office."

"A lawyer? Abducted? Who would abduct a
lawyer? It's like having a rattlesnake for a pet."

"I don't think she's a full-fledged lawyer. I'll find
out."

"What do you know about her at this point?"
the sheriff asked, the corner of his mouth twisted.

"She lived alone, but apparently had a secret
lover, a married man who impregnated her. She
told one of her friends and her sister that he was
going to leave his wife and family and marry her."

Ralph Cutler's eyes widened and then grew
small. He leaned toward McShane.

"Who's the lover?"

"I don't know yet. Not even her sister knew."

"So you went to her apartment?"

"Yeah. There was a set of keys in the purse left
in the car trunk. I didn't find too much. There was
a message on the answering machine from this

girlfriend. I followed up with her, but she couldn't give me much more than I already knew, except to say that she believed Anna Gold's boyfriend was well-to-do."

The sheriff nodded and thought for a moment.

"Did her father know she went and got herself pregnant?"

"No, her sister kept it from him, according to what she told me."

"You sure he never found out?"

"I don't think so, Sheriff. Why?"

"You got to suspect everyone involved in a situation like this."

"I don't know," McShane said, shaking his head skeptically. "I spent some time with the father and sister—"

"About fifteen years ago," the sheriff said, leaning on his elbows on the desk, "there was this teenage girl over in Hurleyville got herself pregnant and wanted to run off with the guy who had done it. Her father got wind of it and went berserk. He caught her, locked her in the car trunk, and drove off to do battle with the boyfriend."

"What happened? I never heard of that case."

"Way before your time. There was this car chase, banging into each other. The father missed a turn on the old river road below Woodridge and went into the Neversink River. He got out, but the car sunk."

"With the girl in the trunk?"

The sheriff nodded.

"You never know what people will do when they're enraged," Cutler continued. "A little paranoia is a good thing, especially for a detective, Jimmy." The sheriff leaned back. "I'll have to call the district attorney and tell him about all this. We'll have to call the FBI, of course. Where's the woman's car?"

"I had it towed to our lot."

"Okay. They'll want to go over it for prints. Well, one good thing's come out of this Shepherds of God mess: The local media is so overwhelmed covering it, they've apparently not gotten wind of Anna Gold's disappearance yet. We have a little breathing time before they make this county sound like the South Bronx."

"Maybe. The supermarket had a little crowd when I arrived. People will be asking questions tomorrow."

"Okay, keep going. I'll speak with Frank Reynolds at the FBI office and see what they want to do. Most likely they'll send someone over here in the morning. Check in with me before I go over to the county supervisor's office."

"Right."

The sheriff stared a moment in thought and then looked at McShane with more sympathy.

"How are things between you and Gayle?"

"Not good."

"Yeah, I heard a little here and there. Bad news

spreads faster than cream cheese around here."

"Anywhere, not just here."

"Well," Ralph Cutler said, folding his hands on his stomach, "keep busy. It's the only remedy to hard times, I find."

McShane smiled.

"That's what got me into trouble in the first place, I think," he said.

The sheriff gazed at the phone.

"Yeah, maybe you're right. We should all remain bachelors until we retire."

McShane laughed and rose.

"See you early in the morning," he said.

"I'll probably not have moved much from where I am right now," Cutler said sadly.

On the way out, McShane stopped at the dispatcher's desk.

"Do me a favor, Marta," he said to the small Hispanic woman manning the phones and radio. He reached into his pocket and produced the other index card he had taken from Anna Gold's desk. It was the one with the cellular phone number. "Get me the name that's behind this number. Leave it on my desk. I'll get it in the morning."

"Cellular," she said immediately when he handed her the card.

"I know."

"They can be hard-asses, demand a paper," she warned. "Demand you show probable cause and go through security."

"Use your charm," he said. She smirked.

"The last time I did that, I got myself stuck with a lazy husband and three children."

He laughed and left the station. On the steps, he paused to gaze at the media that remained: the remotes, the reporters, cameras, microphones. *Maybe all this has come back to bite us,* McShane thought. Criminals, fanatics, terrorists of all sizes and shapes, could utilize the electronic age as well as the police powers utilized it. There had been serial killers in the eighteenth and even the seventeenth centuries, probably serial killers as far back as the caveman days, but they couldn't kill as fast or in as many places then. *The serial killers of the future will probably kill through E-mail,* he thought.

The sheriff was right: To be a good detective, you had to be somewhat paranoid. Everyone was a suspect. Maybe Anna Gold's father had had her abducted, and maybe her older sister, Miriam, didn't know it. Maybe he had heard one of those phone calls Anna made to Miriam. Maybe he had had her kidnapped so he could have her reprogrammed, like those parents who had their kids kidnapped away from cult groups and reprogrammed. To Harry Gold, the outside world was like an evil cult his daughter had joined. Look how he treated her leaving, behaving as though she had died.

No possibility was too far-fetched in today's world, McShane concluded.

And so, maybe he would have to give some credence as well to what he had told the store manager: It was aliens.

He laughed at himself.

"I'm definitely overtired. I've got to get some sleep," he mumbled, and went to his car.

The problem was, he didn't sleep very well in his small apartment. He, like Anna Gold, had fled to claustrophobic quarters, which only served to heighten his isolation. He realized he hated leaving work because that was when he felt most alone now. Of course, Cookie would say it was his work that had isolated her. Now it appeared that his work isolated both of them.

He started the engine and then his stomach churned.

"I forgot to eat," he reminded himself. He would stop at the Monticello diner and grab something fast. He had to get some sleep and be fresh in the morning. There was plenty to do, and besides, he thought, there was a young woman out there being held against her will. She must be very frightened—if she was still alive, that is.

He started to put the car into drive and then paused to reach into the pocketbook beside him on the seat to take out the wallet. He opened it and glanced at the picture of Anna Gold on her license.

Sweet face, he thought, vulnerable. He saw the resemblances between Anna and Miriam and he recalled Miriam holding the Sabbath candle, the light flickering on her face, which would most likely have been serene if his arrival hadn't put the look of fear into her eyes.

He wanted to wipe away that fear almost as much as he wanted to free Anna Gold from her captors, whoever they might be.

And, in a strange way, he thought he might just set himself free in some way as well.

13

He liked the early-morning smell in the hospital after the maintenance people had done their mopping and their dusting. The floors and windows gleamed. As he strode through the entrance to the lab he inhaled the aseptic aromas of cleansing agents, alcohol, and polish. He thought of it as safe. All the germs were dead. He was especially happy for the babies on the maternity floor.

He hated the afternoon smell because it was a composite of unpleasant aromas: blood, phlegm, urine, and stool, as well as the odors visitors brought in with them, especially on rainy days, which today promised to be. On rainy days there was a dank, musty odor visitors tracked over the floors and through the hallways. He thought: On days like this, no one should be permitted in the maternity wing except the nurses with their clean white shoes.

As much as he could, he kept to himself while he worked. He wasn't very good at gossip. His mother used to say that if you talk about someone, it will come back to haunt you somehow, someday. Most of the conversation depressed him anyway. Usually the nurses, the other technicians, even the doctors, talked about their children, their families, vacation plans, holidays, and homes.

He wasn't unpleasant to anyone, and no one had to ask him twice for a favor. He just wasn't anyone's first choice for conversation, not only because he wouldn't gossip, but because his responses to their questions were concise, often monosyllabic. He offered no elaboration. If someone asked him where he had grown up, he replied, "Albany." He didn't describe the neighborhood or the house; he didn't say whether he liked living there or not, and he never volunteered information about his family.

Apparently he hated talking about where he lived now. Everyone thought it was because he was ashamed of it. All they knew was that the place had been in his wife's family for generations, actually going back to the mid-nineteenth century. No one at the hospital had ever visited him or his wife, but most knew that the house was down a side road that turned into a dirt and gravel road. There was no municipal water or sewer, no cable television. He was lucky to have electricity.

He was just as closemouthed when they asked him about his schooling. He didn't seem proud of anything he had done or anyplace he had been. Most important, he rarely if ever asked anyone else any questions about their background. Having a conversation with him was like hand-pumping gasoline into your car.

Everyone simply thought he was shy, but he was good at his work; he was efficient, pleasant to the patients, obedient; he never complained. He treated the doctors and the nurses with the utmost respect. In fact, there was only one thing he did that attracted any attention, and when people found out about his wife's health history, it usually meant he attracted pity as well. All his coworkers knew that, especially on days like this one, when he had a large gap in his workload, he would inevitably wander down to the maternity ward. He would go to the nursery window and look at the babies. When the proud fathers arrived, he would stand beside them.

"I bet I know which one's yours," he would say. It was about the only time he would ever initiate a conversation.

"Really?"

"The boy with the dimple." He pointed to an infant. "Am I right?"

"Yes. How did you know? I don't have any dimples."

"I have this ability to look at a newborn infant and see the parents in his or her face."

"That's incredible. The first day I came here, I

was worried I wouldn't be able to recognize my own kid. All babies look alike to me."

"Oh, but they're not alike. They're different from the moment they're conceived," he told the man, and elaborated on why that was so. It was always the same speech. The excited father would listen and nod. Some were so impressed, they asked him if he was a doctor.

"Hardly," he would say, smiling. "I'm just a leech."

"Leech?"

"I'm a blood technician. I fill the tubes and bring them down to the lab for analysis. Last week I had to do a baby, not much older than the ones you see here. I hate doing babies. I'd hate to think I was hurting a baby."

He actually had tears in his eyes when he said this. The new father was usually touched.

"I know what you mean," he would say. Or: "I can understand that. Got kids of your own?" the man might ask. Many often asked that question. They thought a man with such sensitivity had to have children of his own.

"Not yet," he said, smiling at the babies, "but soon. My wife's pregnant."

"Oh, congratulations."

"Thank you."

"Hoping for a boy or a girl?"

"It doesn't matter."

"I know. It shouldn't. You should just hope the

baby's healthy, but I have to confess I was happy our first was a boy. Carry on the old name, understand?"

"No," he replied, but with a smile. "A baby is his or her own person."

"Right, right."

There was usually a deep silence then. He would look once more at the man's child and then he would walk away, the crying of the babies like music in his ears.

Sometimes, when he came down at night, he felt as if he were the father of each and every one of the babies. He would stand in the window and look at them all, a wide grin on his face. Often, the maternity nurse on duty would invite him to help with the feeding. They all said he was a man with a gentle touch, a man who understood what it meant to nurture an infant. Too bad, they said, that of all men, he was one whose wife had had her ovaries removed.

Recently, following Mommy's orders, he began to speak of their intent to adopt.

"We have to prepare people for the eventuality," she told him, "so they don't wonder how we happened to have a baby."

It was one of the few times he actually initiated conversation with his fellow hospital employees, usually at lunchtime in the hospital cafeteria.

"Congratulations," they told him. Everyone acted as if adopting a baby were the same as having your own.

"We've hired an attorney," he told his coworkers. "It's the best and the fastest way. People who've adopted children have had a lot of trouble these days because they didn't have the right legal foundation. That's not going to happen to us. When we get our baby, he or she will be our baby forever."

"They're not babies forever," Martha Atwood muttered between bites of her sandwich. She conducted EKGs but always looked as though she were on the verge of a heart attack herself. She was forty-one, yet she looked more like sixty with her prematurely gray hair and her deep crow's-feet. When he told Mommy the things she said about her own children and what she looked like, Mommy said Martha Atwood's bitterness was drying her up.

"Martha's right," Tommy Patterson said. He was another lab technician, about twenty-seven, black, and gay.

"How would you know about children?" Martha snapped. She didn't hide her disdain for Tommy's sexual preferences and lifestyle.

"I got younger brothers and sisters. I got a sister just turned twelve."

"How many children did your mother have?" he asked, not hiding his envy.

"Oh, it ain't the same mother," Tommy replied, "but the kids are a handful just the same."

"People shouldn't have children if they don't want them," he said, "for both their benefits."

"Thought you didn't believe in abortion," Martha muttered.

"I don't. I mean they shouldn't conceive."

"Yeah, well, don't you also oppose any form of birth control?" Martha pursued.

"No. I believe in abstention."

"Just say no," Tommy added with a wide smile. "I do it all the time."

"I bet that's the only reason you've never been pregnant," Martha said dryly, and Tommy roared.

He didn't laugh. This was a topic that didn't belong in the realm of humor. As Mommy said, the reason the country was in the moral decay it was in was simply because we weren't taking our responsibilities seriously enough. Teenage pregnancy, the promiscuity of youth, the pornography permitted on television, all of it contributed to the increasing immoral climate.

"You looking for an infant or are you combing foster homes?" Martha asked him.

"We're making arrangements with a young woman who is pregnant but not married."

"Now, that's nice," Tommy said. "It's the way I would go about it. Someday I just might," he threatened, knowing how Martha Atwood would react. Her eyes widened and her lips whitened.

"Gay couples shouldn't have the right to adopt," she declared. "It's enough young people see it out in the open."

"Now, Martha, don't get Neanderthal on me,"

Tommy said, and laughed. Martha muttered under her breath and then turned to him.

"Good luck to you and your wife," she said.

He thanked her.

From time to time Martha, Tommy, or others he had told asked him how it was going. He claimed the arrangements had been made. They were just waiting. All looked well. In the meantime he continued to go down to the maternity floor and look at the babies. When he returned home, he brought descriptions of the babies. At dinner he would tell Mommy about one in particular and she would ask him every day about that baby until the parents took him or her home. He would quickly substitute a new infant in his conversation so Mommy wouldn't be depressed.

However, now that their baby was being made in the basement, he didn't feel as much of a need to bring home descriptions and stories about other infants. Instead he concentrated on how the nurses treated the infants. He asked questions about their rashes and their feeding. He brought home all the pamphlets the hospital provided to new parents.

He also learned as much as he could about pregnancy itself. He went into the pharmacy and pilfered some of the medications Mommy wanted them to have in the house: tranquilizers, magnesium sulfate, and one of the betamimetics, in case there was premature labor.

Whenever he could, he visited the pregnant women on the verge of giving birth. One woman even let him feel her contractions; another told him she wouldn't mind if he attended the actual birthing. He was very excited about that, but when he showed up, the woman's husband objected and he hurried away.

Mommy told him not to worry about the birthing this time, but he couldn't get the pregnant teenage girl's screams out of his head some nights. Some nights, he thought he heard her pleading, crying, wailing through the floorboards again. Her stepfather, a transient hotel worker, had impregnated her. When Mommy had found out, they coaxed the girl away from the trailer home one night when no one was around. She trusted Mommy because she had met her at the doctor's office.

But the girl, her name was Denise, was barely thirteen and the birthing became complicated. Both she and the baby died. It was Mommy's idea for them to take Denise and the dead infant to the old Hillside Cemetery near Mountaindale and bury them in one of the old graves. Who would think to look for dead bodies in a cemetery? Especially one that was no longer cared for and was overgrown. Some of the graves went back to the early 1800s. The cemetery was no longer utilized. Only the real old-timers even knew about it. Everyone else barely glanced at it when he or she rode by and never gave it a second thought.

Mommy assured him things would be different with Anna Gold. She was healthy and certainly old enough to give birth naturally and easily. And besides, she wasn't really the one who was important: Their baby was who was important. After the baby was born, they would keep Anna around as a wet nurse for a few months, she told him.

"And then?"

"And then," Mommy said, "it would be better if we put Anna in the old cemetery too—better for the baby, better for us, even better for Anna."

He agreed, of course. Mommy was usually right about most things. She would make a wonderful mother. He was actually doing what he advised most would-be fathers not to do: He was hoping for a girl. Mommy needed a girl. She had so much to teach a girl. There would be time enough for him to have his son. They had decided only just recently that they would have three children, as long as at least one was a boy.

"They'll learn to love and cherish each other and protect each other," Mommy predicted. "It won't be like your brother or my brother and sister."

Neither he nor Mommy had much to do with their families anymore. The alienation was mutually accepted. It was just painful on holidays.

"Soon, though," Mommy reminded him, "soon we'll have little people for whom to buy presents and decorate a tree and hide eggs."

"And birthdays with candles on the cake."

"And toys, but sensible toys."

"And we'll all go to church."

"And pray together and love one another."

"And be a family," he said.

"Yes," Mommy said. "And be a family."

As he recalled this conversation today, he smiled at the babies through the window. He had come down to maternity during his lunch hour. One of the new fathers joined him. His face was full of pride, his eyes lit like birthday candles.

"Hi," the new father said, bursting with joy.

"I bet I know which one is yours," he said.

And he did.

14

Anna had no way of telling time. The television set only played videos; there was no radio, nor were there windows to let her judge time of day from the sunlight. Her stomach was tied in too tight a knot to telegraph when she had hunger for breakfast or lunch or dinner. She was completely dependent on her captors to know when it was morning, so when her eyes snapped open, she lay there wondering if she had slept through the night or merely a few minutes. It added to the disorientation and anxiety.

She sat up and took some deep breaths. Then she told herself again that she had to get control. She had to find a way to escape. She listened. There was that muffled grinding sound, but otherwise the house was cemetery-quiet. She slipped off the bed and held the chain in her hands so it wouldn't slide over the floor. She didn't want them knowing she was moving about the room yet. That might bring them down.

After she unscrewed the faucet handle, she returned to the hook in the wall and pried at it, again using the handle like a crowbar. She got the hook to make a full turn and then half of another turn before she decided she had better put the handle back and return to bed. They could bust in on her at any moment. Sure enough, only minutes later she heard the key in the door lock. Fortunately, she was in bed. There was no telling what these crazy people would do if they realized she was trying to escape.

The woman entered carrying a breakfast tray. She was still in her own nightgown, her hair looking unkempt, her face pale. She walked with her shoulders and back straight, her lips pressed so tightly they wrinkled and had a thin white line at the corners of her mouth. She had the demeanor of someone who had been in the military, perhaps a military nurse, Anna thought. Maybe, if she got into some sort of conversation with this woman, an opportunity would present itself.

"You have two soft-boiled eggs, wheat toast, orange juice, and coffee with low-fat milk," she recited. "Your vitamin is on the tray."

She put the tray on the night table and stepped back, her hands on her hips.

"It's chilly. Is it raining or anything?"

"I put the heat up a little more," she said. "Yes, it's a nasty day. You're lucky you're inside."

"What time is it?" Anna asked.

"You don't have to know what time it is," she replied. "I'll wake you every morning. I'll bring you your lunch when it's time for your lunch and your dinner when it's time for that."

"Why are you doing this? You can't keep me here all these months," Anna said softly. "People will be searching for me. I promise you, I'm not getting an abortion. I'm going to be married. I won't tell anyone what you did. It's only been a day."

The woman stared at her for a moment as if Anna had presented a viable solution. Then her face returned to its hard look.

"Your eggs and your coffee will get cold. Start eating," she ordered.

"I have no appetite. I feel sick to my stomach."

"That's normal during the first trimester of pregnancy. Don't worry about it. I know exactly what you are going through and will go through, and I know exactly how to care for you."

"How do you know what to do? Who are you? Did you work in a hospital, a clinic?"

"That's not important. What's important is that I will be a real mother to the baby after the baby is born. You should be grateful."

"Grateful!" Anna felt the fury rise in her again

and her cheeks redden. A thought was born. If she could turn them against each other . . . "Do you know what your husband did to me last night?"

"Whatever he did, he had to do. He's a good man."

Anna laughed.

"A good man? A rapist?"

She took a step forward and slapped Anna sharply across her left cheekbone. The blow was so hard, it sent pain down the side of her neck and into her shoulder. Anna cried out and raised her arms to protect herself against another whack.

"You're a whore. You have no right to cast any stones," the woman said. Her pale face had turned a light scarlet and her eyes gleamed with exquisite anger. "You don't even know who the father of that baby inside you is."

"Yes I do," Anna said through her tears. "And he is a man of power and importance. When he finds out what you've done, he'll hunt you down and see that you're both punished."

She smiled and shook her head.

"Idle threats fall on dumb ears. I'll be back in a half hour. If you haven't eaten, I'll tell Daddy to bring back the IV. We'll strap you down and feed you that way for the remaining months. You'll be confined to a bedpan. Do you understand?"

Anna glared back at her. The woman smiled and walked out, locking the door.

She never forgets to do that, Anna thought sadly. She sighed and looked at the tray of food. She needed the juice. Her throat was scratchy, dry. Ironically, the madwoman was right, she thought. She had to eat to maintain enough strength to effect an escape. Her stomach bubbled and twice she thought she would heave, but she managed to get down most of the egg and toast. The coffee was weak and already cool.

After she ate, she went to the bathroom, but she didn't return to the bed. Instead, she walked around the room slowly, inspecting it, looking for some weakness. Something did catch her eye on the far right side. She knelt down and ran her fingers over the scratches. On closer inspection, she realized someone had gouged her name in the wall: *Denise.* Under it were numbers. She studied them, trying to understand what they meant. Date? Time? They had been strung more like serial numbers, more like . . . someone's social security number! she realized. Whoever it was wanted to be certain that whoever found this would be able to identify her.

Anna continued to search the cement until she found more numbers, these looking like dates. If she read them correctly, whoever had scratched them into the wall had done so a little over a year ago.

Could it be that some other poor woman had been imprisoned here? The very thought was terrifying because it would mean that these mad people had done this before and done it without being caught. Then, what happened to the prisoner? Was she a pregnant woman too? Was there a baby? Where's the baby?

That strange, monotonous grinding noise was louder on this side of her cell. She pressed her ear to the wall and listened. It was like a machine that needed lubrication, but there was also the sound of water rushing over rocks.

The key in the door lock triggered her instinctive move to rise to her feet.

The woman was dressed now, her hair brushed back. She wore light lipstick but no eye makeup. In her left hand she clutched a thick, dark brown leather book with a cloth bookmark dangling from between some pages.

"Good," she said looking at the tray. "You ate well. The more cooperative you are, the better things will be for you."

"You've done this to someone else, haven't you?" Anna accused.

The woman stood there, blinking rapidly for a moment. Then she regained her stern composure.

"You should be concerned only with yourself, and you should judge not that ye be not judged. That's from the Bible, which I have brought you. I want you to read it and consider your soul and what you have done to stain it."

"You talk about evil? Look what you're doing," Anna said holding her arms out.

"We're doing good works for which we shall be rewarded."

She put the Bible on the bed and took the tray.

"I have the section marked that I want you to read. If you don't understand it or you have any questions, you can ask me about it later," she said, "when I bring you lunch." She smiled. "Eventually, you will understand and forgive us, just as we have forgiven you."

"I'll never forgive you," Anna said through her clenched teeth.

"I don't like threats," the woman said from the doorway. "And I don't like you festering in a pool of hate. The venom will trickle into the baby and poison her or him. If you don't become pleasant soon, I'll . . ." She smiled. "See to it that you are."

The veiled threat put a chill into Anna, who quickly embraced herself.

"Read those pages and especially the lines I have marked," the woman said, and left.

Anna hurried back to the bathroom and unscrewed the faucet handle. She returned to the hook and pushed and pulled with all her strength, working more furiously now. The hook turned again and again. The wall flaked. She jerked the neck of the hook back and forth, working the hole wider, and then she turned the screw again until she was now able to turn it without the faucet handle. Moments later it came out of the wall. She rejoiced, but smothered her cry of delight. She had mobility. She could wrap most of the chain around her hand and carry it along when she fled this hellhole.

Now, what remained was to work out a way to get out of the room and past this mad couple. But she knew she couldn't let them know she had freed the chain. She put the hook back in the wall, turned it a few times so it was secure-looking, and then cleaned up the chips and the dust beneath it on the floor. Encouraged, hopeful, she sat on the bed.

There was nothing to do now but wait for an opportunity. She opened the Bible to the page the madwoman had bookmarked for her to read and went directly to the underlined passage.

A good tree cannot bring forth evil fruit, neither can a corrupt tree bring forth good fruit.

She immediately thought about the anger in her father's face the day she had left.

"I am not corrupt!" Anna screamed. "I am not corrupt," she muttered through her new tears.

But she had to admit she had slept with a married man, and she had taken his seed into her, and she was locked in this madhouse.

All her tears and shouts wouldn't wipe that fact away.

It weakened her resolve.

Perhaps she deserved all this. Perhaps she shouldn't try to escape.

Perhaps God did send these people.

She sucked in her breath and fought to regain her composure. It was foolish to think like this; it was self-defeating. She had broken with her father precisely because she refused to believe that God kept a scorecard and treated men and women as if they were children. What was happening to her had nothing to do with any divine retribution. The evil on this earth was man-made, not a device for an angry god. . . .

Surely by now many people must realize she was gone and that something terrible had happened to her, she thought. Surely her car in the supermarket parking lot must have created interest and some investigation. She would be found; she would be saved. On Monday everyone in the public defender's office would become concerned too. A massive manhunt would get under way. Potential witnesses would be questioned. Someone might have seen these people abduct her. It was just a matter of time. And if she could just break out of this room . . .

But what if she couldn't? What if she got out of this room only to discover they had locked all the other doors, and what if they stopped her escape? She had no doubt that they would be enraged, even more crazed. There was no telling what they might do. But she had to take that chance. Kidnappers rarely if ever freed the people they abducted. She would die here eventually. She had no doubt of that.

It suddenly occurred to her that on Monday her

father would mark another monthly anniversary of her departure and perform his symbolic mourning. Maybe, she thought sadly, it would soon stop being symbolic.

She took a deep breath and stood up. She had to walk around, keep her body limber. The chain dragged. The collar never felt more oppressive. It seemed to take so much more of an effort to lift her arm and pull the collar away from her throat. Every part of her had gotten to feel so heavy. It was as if they had attached weights to her arms and her legs to slow her movements and prevent any attempt at escape. Even her eyelids were turning into little sheets of steel.

She yawned and then paused to put her hand against the wall to keep her balance.

"What's wrong with me?" she muttered, and stood there thinking about it. Her eyes went wide when she reached an obvious conclusion.

The food! she thought. *They're putting something in the food!* She had to stop eating and drinking what they gave her, but then they would force feed her intravenously. What could she do?

I can flush it down the toilet, she thought, *so they'll believe I've eaten everything.* But then, without any food and water in her system, she would become even weaker and not be able to effect an escape. She couldn't wait long; she had to do this soon.

After taking another deep breath, she made her

way back to the bed. She fought to keep her eyes
open, but they were becoming glued shut, and the
muffled grinding just outside the wall was hypno-
tizing.

I'll just sleep for a little while, she thought, *and
then I'll plan my escape.*

15

When he woke and got out of bed, McShane felt as he imagined Lazarus must have felt, rising from his grave. It had been a mistake to eat dinner so late, and then, afraid he wouldn't fall asleep, he had two stiff bourbons. He passed out watching a documentary on bees on the Discovery Channel, woke, dragged himself to bed, fell asleep, but then woke up what seemed like every twenty minutes. He tossed and turned, unable to find a comfortable sleeping posture. He got up to get a drink of water, took a leak, and minutes later rose to take another leak. Then he tossed and turned until it was nearly morning, when he finally fell into a deep sleep.

The gray skies were gone. He had forgotten to pull down the shades on the two windows on the east side of his tiny bedroom, so the intensifying rays of the rising sun came slicing through the panes, poking at his face until he woke. When his eyes snapped open, he felt as if someone had lifted the lid on his coffin and he was once again confronted with the burden of life.

He scrubbed his cheeks with his dry palms, stretched, coughed, and went to the bathroom. His shower revived him. He thought he actually felt his heart start up like an old car engine, the blood trickling through his veins. When he looked at himself in the mirror, he saw how bloodshot his eyes were and determined he wouldn't take his sunglasses off from the moment he put them on.

The kitchen had always looked like a research lab to McShane. He was a terrible cook and readily admitted he was capable of burning water. The coffee he made for himself never resembled the coffee he made for himself previously. Either he put in too much or too little the next time. Even the idiotproof automated pot didn't stop him from messing up.

Nevertheless, he had to get some caffeine into his blood as soon as possible. He got the coffee going while he dressed, gulped a cup of what tasted more like stale tea, and started out, intending to stop at the diner for some breakfast.

But his phone rang just as he reached the front door of his two-by-four, one-bedroom apartment. It was Cookie.

"Don't you have an answering machine, Jimmy?" she asked, her voice thick with irritation.

"Didn't get a chance to set it up."

"What's there to set up? It's not like taking a year to fix a leak in the faucet," she added, scratching at the scar of an old wound.

"I hate messages. I like full conversations," he quipped. "Why is an answering machine suddenly so important?"

"I tried to get you last night."

"Did you call the station?"

"I don't like calling you at the station. I never did. You know that."

"Well, that's where I work, so that's where I usually can be found." Another old wound. "Whatja want?" Could she have had second thoughts? Was there yet a possibility of another reconciliation? He almost convinced himself he would actually try harder this time.

"I wanted to know why you haven't returned the papers to my attorney. I would like to put this house on the market," she replied, punching a hole in his balloon of hope.

"Really? Why do you want to do that, Cookie? You gotta have a place to live. I thought you liked the house, liked where it was located."

"I can't afford the mortgage on my salary alone and still have money for other things I need. Besides, it's too big for one person. Families live in houses; individuals live in apartments," she said.

"How long are you going to be one person?" he asked. He really wasn't being sarcastic, but she was ready to pounce.

"I've been one person for some time, Jimmy. That's the point."

"All right," he said. There was a dull buzz in his head. "It's early. I haven't had a chance to do more than sip some horrible coffee. I haven't got the strength for this sort of thing."

"Do you have the strength to sign a paper?"

He gazed around the small kitchen. The envelope from her attorney was sitting on the counter, unopened.

"I'll sign the documents and put them right in the mail," he promised.

"Thank you, but don't just tell me you're *going* to do it, Jimmy. *Do* it. If you have to, pretend it has to do with one of your investigations."

"All right, Cookie, I'll do it," he said in a tired, defeated voice. She was quiet.

"What are you doing these days, Jimmy? Are you involved with that horrible incident at the clinic?"

"No. I'm on a missing-person case, a young woman abducted in the Van's Supermarket lot."

"When did that happen?"

"Yesterday," he said. "But it was lost in the commotion after the riot at the clinic."

"How old a woman?"

"Twenty-six, unmarried, but apparently pregnant, with a secret, married lover. Any suggestions?"

"Do you know what happened to her?"

"Not a clue yet, just some theories," he replied. Funny, he thought, when they were living together, she hated asking him questions about his work. Now that they were apart, time and distance gave her the courage to do so. He felt himself sliding away, falling back into the persona of a mere acquaintance. Whatever intimacy they had shared was disintegrating right before his eyes. There was the danger that they would become friends.

"Well, I don't want to keep you from your work, but please send back the papers. Things have to be recorded, and you know how it gets with government agencies. I think I could sell the house fairly soon. Jerry Hampton has a number of buyers he thinks would be interested."

"Okay."

"Take care of yourself," she said. It was the first soft word.

"You too."

He hung up the receiver and stood there a moment, the realization that he had lost something significant, something special, that he might never find again crystallizing. His life flashed before him and he saw himself bouncing from one superficial relationship to another until he found himself alone, a crusty old bachelor sunk in an oversized easy chair in front of a television set, the football games melding into each other until he couldn't distinguish one from the other.

It put him in an even more miserable mood. He

scooped up the manila envelope and started for the door again, and again the phone rang.

"Damn it," he muttered and ripped the receiver from the cradle. "McShane."

"I have Reynolds meeting with you in a half hour in my office," Ralph Cutler said. "Three other pregnant women were abducted this week, one in Dallas and two in Los Angeles. Two were married but were seeking abortions. The FBI is very interested in your case."

"Okay, I'm on my way. I guess you didn't get much sleep, Sheriff."

"At this point my wife wishes it was only another woman," he said. McShane smiled. He really liked Ralph Cutler. He could have been Ralph Cutler, he thought, with a devoted loving wife, a family, a good relationship. Why wasn't it as important to him as it was now, now that he was losing it? It was too hard to think about it.

After he hung up, he realized there wouldn't be enough time to get any breakfast. He went to his cupboard and searched for something resembling edible food. He had bought some chocolate graham crackers and some cold cereals, but he didn't have enough milk. He scooped some of the cereal into a bowl and ate it practically dry. Then he grabbed a chocolate graham cracker and charged out of the apartment. He was nearly to his car before he remembered he had forgotten the manila envelope from Cookie's attorney. He returned, scooped it up again, and left. It lay beside him on the front seat as he drove to the sheriff's office.

Frank Reynolds didn't look like an FBI agent. McShane thought he resembled an accountant. He wasn't particularly tall, maybe five ten, five eleven. He had thinning light-brown hair, wore thick-lens, metal-frame glasses, a dark blue suit and tie, and didn't project a firm, athletic demeanor. He looked like someone who spent most of his waking hours in an office and not in the field. McShane couldn't imagine him putting a suspect under arrest if that suspect offered resistance. Even Reynolds's handshake was a bit limp, tentative. Up until now they had only spoken a few times on the telephone. On the phone Reynolds had a strong voice, but more times than not, people didn't look as you imagined them to be from the sound of their voices. Here, he thought, was a prime example.

"Give him what you've got," Ralph Cutler said, after they were all seated. The sheriff looked the way McShane felt: tired, drawn, on edge.

McShane recited his preliminary investigation. Reynolds sat there with the tips of his fingers pressed against each other, listening. He looked more like someone about to say his prayers. When McShane finished, Reynolds fished a palm-size electronic notebook from his jacket pocket and tapped some keys.

"There were some eyewitnesses to the abduction in Dallas. Two couples were involved. They seized the woman in an underground parking lot immediately after she had seen her doctor at the clinic. It had been her initial visit."

"Clinic?" McShane asked, and looked at the sheriff.

"She was seeking an abortion. The MOs in Los Angeles are similar. You haven't spoken to anyone at the clinic here, I take it?"

"No. I didn't think . . . after what happened yesterday there, I decided I'd wait until today," McShane said, but he didn't believe either the sheriff or Reynolds believed he had given any thought to the possibility that Anna Gold had been seeking an abortion.

"Yes. Well," Reynolds said gazing at the sheriff, "we don't want to create a lot of hysteria here. Next thing you know, there'll be little wars breaking out between the right-to-lifers and woman's rights groups all over the country."

"Seems it's already started," McShane said. "I mean, with the doctor being killed."

"Exactly," Reynolds said. "Anyway, we'll take it from here. You guys have enough to do."

"Amen to that," Ralph Cutler said.

"I'd like to do what I can," McShane said quickly. "I mean, I've met the family. I—"

"Didn't you hear him, Jimmy? This could be a national problem. They have reason to believe these lunatics aren't just protesting clinics and assaulting doctors, they're kidnapping women who seek abortions. It's over our heads. I got a couple of check forgeries I've been sitting on for days. You can get on those."

McShane gazed at Reynolds, who looked as satisfied as a banker who had just closed a great mortgage deal. The man was too businesslike, unemotional. He closed his little electronic notepad and slipped it back into his jacket pocket.

"Just put what you have on paper and I'll get it over to Frank's office later today," Ralph said for Reynolds's benefit.

"Thank you, Sheriff."

"I didn't quite explain this family rift," McShane said.

"Oh, the Jewish problem." Reynolds smiled. "It's not really a major factor here. They're not just after Jews."

"Well, it still could be important. I mean, what if this is an isolated incident and not part of this overall national conspiracy you guys suspect? I mean—"

"I think we'll figure out pretty quickly if it's part of the pattern," Reynolds offered. He stood. "For now, Sheriff," Reynolds said, turning away from McShane, "I would suggest you refer all media inquiries concerning the woman's disappearance to our office. In light of what happened at the clinic, we've got to handle this delicately."

"Glad to get it off my back."

Reynolds smiled.

"That's what we're here for: to help you local police agencies when it becomes necessary. Detective," he said, offering his hand again. McShane rose.

"If there is any detail you want me to elaborate on later . . ."

"Oh, we'll call you, Detective. One thing about the FBI: We're not shy." He smiled at the sheriff, who nodded and laughed.

"Get right on your report, will ya, Jimmy."

"Okay," McShane said. He paused, but it was obvious Reynolds wasn't going to leave the office before he did.

"These other cases," McShane asked, "were any of the women rescued?"

"Not yet. It's all happened very quickly. That's why we need to get on this one as soon as possible."

"Jimmy?" the sheriff said. McShane nodded and left the office.

As he sauntered down the corridor toward his office and desk, McShane felt an emptiness in his stomach that he knew was precipitated by more than the lack of good food. He couldn't get Miriam Gold's eyes out of his mind. He felt as if he were deserting her and, more important, deserting her sister. The FBI, Reynolds in particular, was too concerned about the political ramifications of this thing. And these federal agencies saw conspiracies everywhere. Talk about your paranoia: They had it on a grand scale. What usually happens, McShane thought, is that the individual victim gets thrown into a pile of statistics. There wasn't enough concern about the poor woman. Where was she? What were they doing to her?

At his desk he put a sheet of paper into the typewriter and began his report. His phone rang. He kept typing after he stuck the receiver between his ear and shoulder and said, "McShane."

"This is Miriam Gold," she said. He stopped typing.

"Yes, ma'am. I'm afraid I don't have much to tell you yet," he said.

"I didn't think so, but I have something I have to tell you. I . . ."

"Yes?"

"I was reading this morning's paper . . . this whole business at the clinic, the killing of Doctor Williams . . . horrible."

"Yes, it is."

"I didn't tell you everything yesterday. I was ashamed. It was foolish of me."

"Ma'am?" His heart began to pound in anticipation.

"My sister was considering the possibility of an abortion. She met with Doctor Williams. I wasn't much help to her, I'm afraid. I don't know if this means anything. . . ."

"It could," McShane said sadly. "The case is being turned over to the FBI. There have been some similar cases in other states recently."

"Oh."

"I'm sure they'll be contacting you," he added.

"Then, you won't be involved?"

"Only tangentially," he said. "But you can't ask for more than having the FBI on it."

"Yes," she said. And then she added, "I'm sorry I held back information."

"It's all right. Thanks for the call," he said, and she said good-bye, her voice drifting away like a leaf in the wind.

He sat there with the receiver in his hand, thinking. It felt as if he had just told someone her sister had the worst possible disease, maybe cancer. If Anna Gold were indeed another victim in a nationwide conspiracy, she had been abducted by more sophisticated people with more resources available to them. It made it harder and it filled him with rage. He wished he could pursue these fanatics and not just hand it over to the FBI.

He completed his report, adding the content of Miriam Gold's recent call to the end of it. Then he brought it and Anna Gold's pocketbook with all its contents to the sheriff. He told him about the phone call he had just received from Miriam Gold.

"So this thing does look like something bigger," Ralph Cutler said.

"Maybe."

"Not our problem now. Okay, look into those forgeries. See Steve Powell at the First National Bank first thing tomorrow."

"Right."

"Jimmy," Ralph said as McShane started away. McShane turned. "One of the first things I learned when I got into this business is I couldn't save everyone and I should get used to the idea."

"Funny," McShane said. "I always knew that to be true, but I always thought we should go at it as if we thought we could."

"That's a young, inexperienced man's philosophy."

"Maybe just an idealist," McShane said.

"Same thing," the sheriff retorted. McShane shrugged.

"I guess you're right, Sheriff, but it's sure depressing to be right sometimes."

Ralph nodded and McShane left, never feeling more frustrated about himself and the work he had chosen to do.

16

It happened to her faster this time. With the last two human incubators, it had taken nearly two weeks; but there was something about this one, something about its resistance and the way it looked back defiantly at her, that accelerated the feeling, the need to think of it as nothing more than a nest in which the fertilized egg developed. She wanted to forget its name and especially its face so she could wipe away the idea that this was another human being. She could do that. Daddy made it possible for her to do that after the second incubator had become rebellious and had cursed her and spit at her.

She had told him she didn't want that creature downstairs to be a person anymore.

"I can't stand looking at its face, Daddy. It glares at me so hatefully, even when it's asleep."

He thought a moment, nodded, and said, "I'll fix that, Mommy. Don't worry."

"What will you do, Daddy? We can't do anything to harm her until after the baby is born."

"I know. Just give me a chance to surprise you," he said. "I have an idea."

He smiled that handsome smile of his that had drawn her to him in the first place.

"What's your idea, Daddy?"

"Be patient," he said, and planted a kiss on her forehead.

She waited, but asked him about it first thing the next day when he came home from work.

"Patience," he reminded her, still with that warm smile she loved.

"You know I hate surprises, Daddy. Most of my surprises were always bad ones," she warned.

"This won't be a bad one."

The next day he looked like the cat that had eaten the canary. Before she could ask anything, he put up his hand and said, "Tomorrow."

And the day after, just as he had vowed, he came home with his surprise. He had had a friend make it in his metal shop, and he had put it in a box and gift-wrapped it with pretty metallic paper filled with promises written in bright silver: *I promise to love you forever. I promise to make you happy. I promise to fill your face with smiles. . . .*

"Go ahead, unwrap it," Daddy said when she just stood there dumbfounded.

She did so as neatly as she could. She wanted to save the promises. Then she opened the box, cleared away the tissue paper, and took it out.

"Well?" Daddy said. "What do you think?"

The solution was so simple, she wondered why she hadn't thought of it herself.

"It's wonderful, Daddy. You didn't let me down."

Now it was in its box on the bedroom closet floor where they had left it after the second incubator died that horrible death.

She stood in the bedroom doorway and looked down at the box. By now the new incubator was asleep. It was a good time. Daddy would be surprised she had resorted to it so quickly, but he wouldn't be upset. He understood. No one understood her as well as Daddy did.

She knelt down, uncovered the box, and plucked it out. She held it in her hands for a moment and then checked to see if the key was where it had been left in the box as well. It was. She would unlock it after this incubator had served its purpose, and put it back in the box to use again with the next incubator. Their plans called for at least two, maybe three more.

This was a perfect size, she thought, amazed at how light it really was. It wasn't too small, nor was it too big. Food and drink could easily pass through the mouth, and the eyes were large enough for the incubator to see what it had to see, without her having to look at those hateful orbs, she thought. There were just two small holes for the ears, but they sufficed.

Once, even before they had put it on the second incubator, she had put it on herself just to be sure it would work. She wasn't happy about wearing it. Her face became a little warm, but she was confident it would in no way endanger the baby growing in the incubator. Ultimately, that was the essential test for anything they would do: Would it be good for the baby?

Well, as long as there was defiance and hate, as long as there was resentment and conflict between her and the incubator, the baby was in some jeopardy. Daddy's surprise gift would once again subdue the rancor and create a neutral atmosphere, at least as far as she was concerned. She wouldn't have to face the sneers, the fire in the eyes, the clenched teeth. Most important, she would have no nightmares.

We should have done it the moment we brought this new incubator here, she thought. *Both Daddy and I were so excited, we didn't think clearly, otherwise we would have.* Convinced she would be doing the right thing for herself as well as for the baby, she left and took it down to the basement. For a few moments she lingered outside the door and listened. The silence convinced her this was her opportunity.

Sure enough, when she opened the door, the incubator's eyes were closed; it was lying on its back on the bed, which was perfect, and it was breathing softly, it chest lifting and falling in a stable rhythm, indicating it was asleep. The tranquilizers were working well.

Making as little noise as she could, practically tiptoeing over to the bed, she gently lifted the incubator's head. Then she slipped it under the head and over the incubator's face and quietly, gracefully, clicked in the two sides to lock it. That done, she lowered the incubator's head to the pillow again and stepped back.

It was like looking at the white wall. Immediately she felt a wave of deep relief crawl through her body, washing away the tension and unhappiness. A new confidence came over her.

"This time we're doing it all right," she muttered. "We won't make any tragic mistakes."

Proud of herself for taking intelligent action, she left the basement bedroom and went upstairs to prepare dinner. They would have a special dinner tonight, a celebration. There would be duck à l'orange and rice and cranberry sauce, champagne and strawberry shortcake with French-roast coffee. Tonight they would dine instead of eat. Their glasses would clink and their laughter would reverberate through this otherwise dank, dark, sad house, a house that had been without children for years.

They would bring the sunshine back in here. It would be warm again, with a fire in the fireplace, the delicious aromas of food permeating every room, the chandeliers sparkling, candles glittering in the old and very valuable antique silver candelabra.

Afterward she might even make Daddy happy by polishing his pendulum with her body oil. She didn't do that too often these days. When she was unhappy, it was hard for her to make Daddy happy, but tonight she was positive she would.

She went about preparing the dinner, humming some quaint tune that lay in her memory like the pale yellow page of an old newspaper in a trunk stored in the attic. She couldn't remember many words, nor could she recall the title of the song, but she vaguely remembered her mother humming it to her when she was having a soft time. That was how she recalled the few-and-far-between happy moments with her mother: soft times; times when her mother forgot how much she resented her birth and the added burden it had brought; times when her mother permitted some love to trickle out from under that mask of unhappiness.

These days she had trouble recalling her mother's face. The oil paintings and photographs in wood frames of her parents and her mother's parents lined the entryway of the old house, but the entryway was not well lit. The wall lamps no longer worked and there were no windows on the door. The door was made of cherry wood. It was chipped and cracked, wrinkled like an old woman, but still strong enough to withstand the weather and the ravages of time.

Sometimes she thought the house looked arthritic. The porch sagged on the right, shingles hung loosely. It was in dire need of a paint job, and the roof leaked in little places. She couldn't remember when she had been in the attic last, but she knew that everything up there was damp and soggy and there were and had been a continuous society of chipmunks and other sorts of rodents residing in its corners and nooks. Often, when the house was quiet, she could discern their tiny feet scratching the attic floorboards as they scurried around the old furniture, trunks, piles of books, and discarded papers that marked the history of her family.

It went back to the Revolutionary War. One of her ancestors, Steven Corning, had been given a tract of land as payment for his participation in the war, and the land had remained in the family ever since. Her brother and sister were more than happy to leave it to her. The called it the Rattrap. They had hated living here so far away from other children, but she had always enjoyed the seclusion and never really cared about what her school friends thought.

When Daddy first saw the house and the grounds, and saw where it was all located, he was sincerely excited about it. She had feared that he, like all the men she had met, would find it odd that she could live there alone all that time, but he completely understood. He was at home here almost immediately, and almost immediately she felt he was the man who would be her husband.

They had met at the hospital. He would often say, "I took your blood but I was really after your heart."

They had struck up a good friendship quickly, and he came around often to visit, stopping every time he was anywhere near her room at first, and then coming when he was off duty. He was the one who would bring her home when she was released, and that was when he first set eyes on the house.

"I never dreamt it would be exactly as you described," he told her. "This is like walking through the wall of time, being protected by time. I love it. It's . . . magical. And you," he said, turning back to her, "you're magical too."

She thought that if a man could love her and want to be with her after what had happened to her, then he must be a good man, and a good man made a good father. She confessed her dreams and he confessed his, which to her required a deeper sense of trust than mere romantic love. They fed each other's hope, and when they talked about what was happening to families around them, they soon saw that they agreed on most of the essential things.

Daddy was the one who suggested they bring the first incubator here. She didn't agree or disagree immediately, but she didn't oppose him when he began the construction of the maternity room downstairs in the basement. He told her he had often had dreams about it, and the dreams were so vivid, he actually thought the room had already been constructed. He said he believed someone had once lived down there anyway.

She turned away, amazed. When she had been little, that was where she had spent all of her private time. Her brother and sister hated the dark, damp basement, where field rats, mice, and snakes dwelled. She had always had an affinity for animals and even people whom other people avoided. The qualities that annoyed, frightened, or disgusted them were qualities that appealed to her. She sympathized with loneliness and fear: She felt it so often herself.

But all that was in the past. She was happy now. She and Daddy again were trying to have a child and raise a family. They desperately needed a family, needed someone else to depend on them, needed a place in which to deposit the love they had bursting inside them. They resented the fact that other people who had so little love to give small people still were able to have small people.

"They pop them out after Lamaze or with painkillers swimming through their veins, and then they immediately hire a nanny until their child is old enough to be put in day care or preschool," he lectured.

She agreed: It was unfair. There were too many things that happened in this world that were unfair. Daddy nodded and his eyes grew small with determination.

"We have to do something about that," he said. "We can't just sit here and watch all this unroll on television and read about it in the papers and shake our heads."

"Yes," she said. She loved when he talked like that, full of passion and anger.

"A child is your child because you love him or her. That's what connects you. People who have children of their own but don't give them any love don't really have children. You understand what I mean, don't you?" he asked.

Of course she did. She understood that even before he had.

"I mean, if we have a child somehow and we give that child our love, it will be our child."

"Yes," she said. "It's all waiting here."

She pressed her hand against her heart.

He smiled and, shortly afterward, went downstairs into the basement and began to build the room. She would often stand by and watch him or hand him a tool. When it was completed they celebrated, just as they would celebrate tonight. They had a wonderful meal and talked softly and she made him happy.

Time passed. It took so long to find the proper first incubator. She used to go downstairs and stare at the empty room and sigh. Daddy knew how sad she was, so he tried harder, and when the opportunity came, he couldn't wait to rush home to tell her.

"We're going to have a baby," he said.

What a wonderful thing to hear; what a wonderful thing for him to have said.

But it didn't happen the way they had hoped.

And it didn't happen the second time either.

But three was always a lucky number for her. This time it was going to happen.

"We're going to have a baby. We're really going to have a baby."

And so she hummed as she worked.

The phone rang. It was Daddy.

"I'm just about finished with my lunch break," he said. "I had to eat later today, so I thought I would call you now to see if there was anything we needed before I checked out for the day."

She thought a moment and smiled to herself, just knowing what the effect of her words would be.

"I'm almost out of my body oil, Daddy," she said. "Could you stop and get me another bottle?"

"Of course I could," he said, the higher pitch in his voice revealing his anticipation. "I guess everything is all right there."

"You guess right, Daddy. Hurry home."

"A team of wild horses couldn't stop me," he said, and she laughed. It was more like a teenager's giggle.

"No groceries?"

"No. I checked. We have everything else that we need for a while."

"Okay. See you soon, Mommy."

Daddy said good-bye and hung up quickly.

Back in the hospital corridor near the pay phone, he stood simmering with glee.

"Who's that you were talking to?" Tommy Patterson asked.

He spun on him as if he had been pricked in the spine.

His fellow lab technician had his head tilted, his face twisted in a smile of curiosity.

"What?"

"I thought I heard you call the person Mommy. Your mother here?"

"You shouldn't eavesdrop on someone else's conversations," he said indignantly.

"I wasn't. I was just passing by and overheard. Don't get your testosterone up."

Daddy cooled quickly and gazed around to be sure no one else had heard. Making a scene always drew more attention to something you didn't want other people to notice.

"It's my wife," he confessed softly, his eyes down. "I do that to make her feel good. You know, with the adoption being set up and all."

"Oh." Tommy smiled. "That's nice. I'm happy for you guys. No two people deserve to have a child more."

"Thank you," he said. He brightened, thinking about how he would tell Mommy what Patterson had said.

"Good luck," Tommy added, and walked off.

He watched him disappear down the corridor. Then he thought about the body oil and Mommy's wonderful hands and the happiness that waited for him at home.

It was really going well. It was going better than ever. This time it was definitely going to happen.

17

For a long moment McShane sat in his car in the sheriff's department parking lot, just thinking about what little he had accomplished on this missing woman case before having to turn it over to the FBI. He felt like someone without a destination, without a purpose.

It was Sunday, and lately Sundays were the loneliest days. Before his separation, when he wasn't working and he was home, he and Cookie would at least enjoy a big breakfast together. Usually he would go out for fresh bagels, usually him while she prepared the omelets. He'd get the Sunday papers and they would eat and read the papers and relax. By late morning, if they didn't go to her parents or have some other destination, he would plant himself in his overstuffed chair before the television set and watch football, baseball, basketball, or golf. Whatever was in season or whatever he could find usually sufficed.

During the early days of their marriage, Cookie often watched with him and asked questions. She would curl up beside him on the sofa and doze or she would bring out her schoolwork, her reports, and work on them while he sat mesmerized by events on the small screen.

After a while the noise, his shouts and comments, began to annoy her. She couldn't work in that atmosphere, and if he had any friends over, it was even worse. On those days she would go visit her friends or her parents and it started to be that they didn't see each other for most of Sunday, meeting finally in the late afternoon or early evening to go to dinner. Many times, however, he was on duty over the weekend, and even the Sunday dinners were lost.

It was actually true that for McShane the weakening and eventual death of his marriage was insidious. Whether it was his work or his many distractions that prevented him from seeing the breakdown, he didn't know, but he was blind to it. The first time Cookie complained with any vehemence, he was sincerely surprised. Somehow he was under the impression that she accepted their marriage as it was. She was annoyed with him at times, sure, but he believed that came with the territory. All of his fellow law enforcement officers had similar experiences, but as far as Cookie feeling deep pain? Never.

The more she pointed out and complained about, the more he fled from her and the worse it became. She called him an ostrich, pounced on his rationalizations, his excuses, and his apologies. She diagnosed his classical avoidance of responsibility and, like a hawk, she spotted every infraction, every minor failure, every unrequited promise, every failed obligation.

When she nailed up the small blackboard in the kitchen and chalked in his every screwup, no matter how minor, his embarrassment turned to irritation. It was like getting a report card. He attributed that to her educator's mentality and he actually stopped going into the kitchen, bringing home snacks from fast-food restaurants instead. Again she pointed her finger and accused him: "Avoidance. Choose the easiest way out, Jimmy. You always do."

He sulked, but then he began to wonder if she could be right. Was that something he always did? As he sat there thinking about it now, his gaze went to the manila envelope on his seat. He opened it and took out the documents, perused them, and found where he was to sign each. After a deep sigh of resignation, he plucked his pen from his inside pocket and scribbled his John Hancock wherever so indicated. Then he shoved the documents back into the envelope.

He started the engine.

He could go home. It was Sunday. He had the rest of the day off, now that the FBI had taken over the investigation of Anna Gold's abduction. The forgeries he was assigned couldn't be followed up until Monday because he had to go to the bank.

He glanced at the envelope again and then made a snap decision and drove out of the parking lot. Now that he had time on his hands and wasn't eager to return to his two-by-four apartment, he would do one good deed: He would hand deliver the signed papers to Cookie.

It was curious the way he felt when he pulled into what had once been his driveway. Cookie hadn't done anything different with the house over this short period, save to put up the real estate broker's FOR SALE sign on the front lawn, yet something of his old home's familiarity was already gone. Somewhere in his glove compartment he might have another key to the front door, but using it now was the equivalent of breaking and entering. This house was as forbidden to him as anyone else's, he thought.

He got out slowly and paused to gaze around, suddenly fascinated by the surroundings. It wasn't that the woods and fields had changed so much as he had never really appreciated them. Because they had built their house a little over a half of a mile from the hamlet and had a good two acres of land, there was a peacefulness, a serenity, around them. They didn't have municipal sewerage but a septic tank, and they didn't have municipal water: They had to have a submersible well. But they had cable television, which had been more important to him at the time.

Cookie made fun of that.

"You'd live in an outhouse as long as you could get ESPN, Jimmy."

He had laughed when she said it, but he couldn't laugh about that now. Maybe his priorities were screwed up, or maybe he was just feeling sorry for himself today. Like any poor schnook involved in a divorce, he was feeling like a loser. Surely this feeling would pass. Or maybe Cookie was right: Maybe he always saw himself as some kind of loser and retreated into the comfort of mediocrity, never challenging, never pushing too hard, never seeking advancement either in his marriage or his profession.

This divorce could be a wake-up call. Would he change? *Change to what?* he wondered. *I am who I am,* he thought. *There's really not much I can do about it except find someone else who's not unhappy with what I have to offer.* Still, he couldn't help wishing he hadn't lost Cookie.

He rang the doorbell, something he realized he had never done. A few moments later all five feet ten inches of her stood before him, those long legs and that tight butt encased in tapered dungarees. She was barefoot, her toenails polished a bright pink. That always bugged him. Most of the time women had their feet covered. Why did they bother polishing toenails?

Cookie wore one of his New York Giants T-shirts, the sleeves rolled up to her shoulders. Her perky breasts lifted the letters. Her hair was brushed back and tied with a light-blue ribbon, a shade lighter than her cobalt eyes. She had that number-two pencil stuck in her hair, so he knew she was working on her reports. She never put the pencil behind her ear. It always stuck up like a hairpin.

Cookie was pretty and not in a cutesy way. She had classic features, a strong, straight nose just a trifle too big, with a firm mouth whose slightly puffed lips were tantalizing. He loved the way her jawbone gently lifted toward her perfect ears, making her cheeks smooth. Except for a tiny patch of freckles under her right temple, she had a nearly clear alabaster complexion. It wasn't hard to understand why, when he had first set eyes on her, he had rushed at her like a defensive tackle intending to sack the quarterback.

Right now, seeing how beautiful she was made him feel as if he had a small ice cube traveling through his heart. He didn't have to wonder any more if there was another man in her life, because if there wasn't one today, there would surely be one here tomorrow.

"What?" she said sharply.

"You opened that door pretty fast," he chastised. "You should be more careful. It's the times we live in, I'm afraid," he added, thinking about Lidia Ambrook standing in her doorway with a Taser in her right hand.

She smirked.

"I saw you drive up, Jimmy. I was working in the den."

"Oh. Right," he said.

"So?"

"I got your papers here," he said, holding up the envelope. "I thought since it's Sunday and the post office is closed, I'd just pop by and drop them."

"You're not working?"

"No. I'm off the big case. Sheriff put me on some forgeries and I can't do anything with that until tomorrow. Bank's closed," he added, stating the obvious.

"No important ball games?" She softened when he smirked. "You don't know what to do with yourself, do you, Jimmy?" she asked perceptively. It bothered him how sharp she was sometimes. *There's great danger in marrying a woman who is a lot smarter than you are,* he thought.

"I just thought, since I didn't get the papers back as promptly as I was supposed to that . . ."

"All right," she said. "Thanks." She took the envelope and then stared at him a moment. "You look lousy, Jimmy. Like you slept in your clothes and didn't have any real breakfast."

He shrugged.

"I feel . . . lousy," he admitted. His failure to put up an argument brought a smile to her face. She folded her arms under her breasts.

"Why did they take you off the case?"

"It's a complicated mess," he said.

She stared a moment. He felt like a little boy trick-or-treating on Halloween.

"You want some lunch, Jimmy?" she asked. "I was about to put in a pizza."

His eyes widened and brightened.

"Sure. Thanks."

She stepped back and he entered what had recently been his home.

"I'm just going to put this in the den," she said, holding up the envelope. She went to the left and he paused at the living room doorway.

To him it felt weird standing there, looking at his overstuffed chair, at the settee, the coffee table, the fireplace and mantel, where some of the small things he had left there still remained. It looked frozen in time. It was almost as if he had died and returned in a different body.

"That mess at the clinic is all over the local news," Cookie said, returning. "Word's leaking out that the FBI think it ties in with some sort of national conspiracy."

She paused to look at him to see if he would comment.

"Yeah, it's possible," he said.

"Really? Why would the lunatic fringe of the religious right target a community smaller than most cities? What's that clinic do, a dozen abortions a month?"

He followed her into the kitchen. That notorious blackboard was gone.

"Maybe they went after it for that reason."

"Huh?"

She took out the frozen pizza and turned on the oven.

"These radicals want to show that no one, no matter how small or how remote, is safe from what they called divine retribution."

She thought a moment and nodded.

"Could be. Want a beer?"

"Sure. Thanks," he said.

"Left over from the cases you bought," she reminded him, and took out a can. She gave him a glass and then took out the plates, knives, and forks. He sat at the table and poured his beer into the glass.

"So, if it's so important a case, why did they take you off?"

"FBI," he said, as if that was all he needed to say. She nodded.

"You can't assist? You have before, haven't you? At least, that's what you used to tell me."

"And I did. No one asked this time."

"Did you volunteer?"

"I did, but the sheriff wasn't in the mood to keep me on it since the FBI was involved. He's feeling put-upon these days and not very generous. The supervisors are calling him on the carpet to find out how this demonstration took place so unexpectedly.

Everyone was caught with his pants down, apparently, and someone's got to be in the hot seat."

He sipped his beer.

"What about the missing woman?"

He shook his head.

"How do you feel about being taken off the case, Jimmy?" she asked with the all-too-familiar psychoanalytical face, her eyes piercing as she waited to weigh his words.

"I don't know. I guess I should be relieved."

"Aren't you?" she fired back, those eyes of hers quickly filling with fire, burning into him.

"I have to follow orders," he said. She smirked.

"Why is it all you quasi military types have the same excuse?"

"It's no excuse," he said, raising his arms. "I'm not the one who decides."

She shook her head.

"How far did your investigation go? Did you get to meet the young woman's family?"

"Yeah, father and a sister. Mother died recently."

"Is that the complicated mess you mentioned?"

"No."

"Top secret?"

"For your ears only," he said, took a swig of his beer, and then added, "FBI believes her abduction has something to do with the clinic riot."

"Really? Why?"

"As I told you on the phone, Anna Gold was pregnant. Her sister admitted Anna had gone to the clinic to see about an abortion. FBI says similar abductions happened to three other women in Texas and California recently."

"When was she scheduled for an abortion?"

"I'm not sure if she had actually scheduled herself. She believed—believes, I should say—her secret lover will want to leave his wife and marry her. Maybe under those circumstances, she wouldn't go for the abortion."

"Of course, her lover could have wanted her to have an abortion whether they got together or not. Some men just don't want the responsibility of a family, as we know," she said, glancing at him quickly, "but she could have also been having some doubts and didn't want to find herself a single mother on welfare, which could happen, especially with the estrangement she had with her family. She was sort of between a rock and a hard place."

Cookie continued: "Did her sister tell you who the secret lover is?"

"No. She didn't know."

"Didn't know?"

"Yeah."

"Anna didn't have a good relationship with her?"

"Well, that's where it does get a little more complicated," he said, and described Harry and Miriam Gold and what had happened to alienate Anna Gold and her father.

Cookie listened, asked for a few more details about Anna Gold, and then took the pizza out of the oven. She cut the slices and put his on a plate.

"What about friends: Maybe one of them knows."

"Maybe. I visited with one who had left a message on her answering machine, but she seemed reluctant to give me a name, violating some feminine trust, I suppose."

Cookie smirked.

"You probably came on like a sledgehammer."

"I told her how serious it was, but she's a kook, into astrology. She's probably consulting the stars to decide."

"Why don't you just go back and calmly explain why you need a name. Give her the details, treat her like an equal, treat her with some respect."

"Pop psychology again?"

"Maybe, but it works."

She ate and thought for a few moments, and he did the same.

"If these fanatics kidnapped her to keep her from aborting, they'll have to keep her incarcerated for months, and then . . ." She looked at McShane, who blew on his piece of pizza.

"What?" he asked.

"Have any of the other women the FBI described been found?"

"Not yet."

"I suppose then it's no different from any other kidnapping. The victim might know too much to be set free, right?"

He chewed and nodded.

"You have no leads?"

"Not really. I just got started when the FBI stepped in and took over."

"If you were still on the case, what would you do next, Jimmy?"

"Well, there's a cellular number I wanted to have checked out. There was no name, just a number. Her apartment was so sparse, there wasn't much else I spotted. Of course, I didn't cut open the mattress. Anyway, I found the number in her Rolodex, along with this friend Lidia Ambrook's number and address. Now that you've given me instructions on how to interview, I suppose I should go back to Lidia Ambrook and try a softer, more reasonable approach," he said, smiling. He mulled a moment. "As far as her being the victim of the lunatic fringe, the FBI usually keeps track of suspicious characters, and would know if any who are connected to this sort of thing are in our area."

"Would they tell you?"

"Yeah, I suppose, or they might say, 'Don't worry about it, we're on it,' like they did."

Cookie ate and thought.

"Who knew Anna Gold was pregnant?"

"Far as I can tell, just her sister and, I imagine, her lover. If Lidia Ambrook knows the lover's name, she might know Anna's pregnant. I haven't interviewed people at the public defender's office, where she worked. Might be someone there."

"Her sister didn't tell anyone?"

"Doubt it. She was so ashamed of it, she didn't tell me about it when I spoke with her the first time."

"People don't exactly pour out their hearts to you the first time they meet you, Jimmy."

"This woman did," he insisted.

She raised her eyebrows and then took his can of beer and poured what remained in her glass. It brought a smile to his face, remembering how she had listed the only two occasions she would drink beer. One was with pizza, the other was with a cheeseburger. Otherwise it was chardonnay.

"Could someone have been watching the clinic to report on who goes in and out?"

"Possible, I suppose, but this clinic's out of town. Anyone loitering nearby would be noticed after a while."

"What about someone there reporting to the Shepherds of God—a spy for the fanatics?"

"Possible," he agreed. "I'd have to question the employees, do some background checks."

She stared at him a moment.

"Sounds like you know where to go, what to do."

He nodded.

She put down her glass and leaned toward him.

"How can you just turn this over to the FBI, Jimmy?" she demanded. "You know people and places here better than some agents sent in from Washington. Every minute is probably critical for this abducted woman. She has to be living in some sort of abject terror."

"I told you—"

"You're not doing anything worthwhile with yourself today, Jimmy. Why not keep on it for free?"

"Sure, now that you're divorcing me, you don't care how I spend my free time."

"I care enough about you still to want you not to waste it, not to waste anything that might give you more confidence in yourself. The worst that can happen is, you find something else to give to the FBI."

"That's not the worst that could happen. The sheriff took me off the case," he protested, but he didn't like the sound of his voice himself. It was a whine.

"You're not doing it for the sheriff, or the county, or even the country, Jimmy. You're doing it for Anna Gold," she said. "My God, Jimmy, don't you ever get tired of taking the easy way out?"

He stopped chewing.

"That's not fair, Cookie. I told you, it's not by choice that I'm off the case."

"I know. It's by acquiescence," she retorted. "Whatever-you-say McShane rides again: 'I'm just following orders.' How convenient."

"Jesus." He slammed down his glass. "Throw me out of the marriage and now get me fired."

"Sorry," she said after a moment. She relaxed her shoulders and sat back. "You're right. It's not fair. I was just thinking about that poor, frightened woman locked up with some fanatics. If it was happening to me, I wouldn't want to know I was being passed around from one law enforcement agency to another while precious time was lost."

"The FBI's pretty good, Cookie. They usually get their man."

"I know, but often it's too late for the victim."

He sat back and gulped the remainder of his beer before standing.

"Well, thanks for the lunch," he said. "And the pep talk," he added.

She laughed and stood, her face turning serious.

"I'm sorry, Jimmy. I never meant for us to end up like this."

"Me neither."

They stared at each other for a moment and then he turned and walked out of the house, trying desperately not to look back.

The peaceful scene that greeted him outside his former house reminded him of the tranquility he had found at the Golds' residence in Parksville. The madness around them had descended like some disease; it recognized no boundaries.

Cookie's words resounded in his ears. He almost didn't hear his beeper go off.

"There goes my free time," he muttered, and went quickly to his car radio.

It was Marta.

"I just found out you're off today," she said, "but

I got the information you wanted and I thought you might find it very interesting."

"Information?"

"That cellular telephone number?"

"Oh, yeah. Why's it interesting?"

"It belongs to Robert Royce."

"Robert Royce?"

"Don't you read the papers?" She laughed. "Weren't you here last night?"

"I give up," he said. "Who the hell is he?"

"He's Gault's attorney—Gault, the leader of the Shepherds of God."

"Really?" He thought a moment. "Thanks, Marta."

He sat back in his seat. Why would Anna Gold have his cellular number?

He looked back at his former home. He thought he saw Cookie in the den, hovering over her computer keyboard. She was a dedicated, determined person. He was beginning to understand why his laid-back style had become abhorrent to someone so goal-oriented.

"Oh, what the hell," he muttered. "There's nothing really good on television anyway."

He started the engine and backed out of the driveway, suddenly rather pleased with the prospect of doing something more than he had to do.

18

Anna woke with a start and then blinked rapidly. At first, unaware of what had been done to her, she was confused by her narrowed vision. *Am I still asleep?* she wondered. *Am I dreaming?*

It looked and felt as if she were gazing up from the bottom of a grave. Slowly, baffled, she brought her hands to her face. When they made contact with the cold metal mask, she gasped and sprang into a sitting position so quickly that the chain connected to the collar around her neck rattled and flew over her shoulder. What had been done to her? What was this? She moved her hands all around her head, and then she screamed.

Her cry echoed inside the mask, reverberating through her skull and bouncing down her spine. Despite the excruciating effect, she screamed again and then she pried her fingers under the mask and began to tug with all her strength, hoping to rip it off, but it didn't move.

Her gasping grew more intense, along with the pounding of her heart. A pain shot across her chest and wrapped itself with the sting of barbed wire around her ribs, closing, tightening, forcing her to take smaller and smaller breaths. Panicking, she clawed again and again at the mask, pulling at the mouth, the eye holes, even trying to widen the openings for her nostrils.

"I'm going to suffocate to death," she cried.

Although the mask was only around her head, the effect was to make her feel as though her whole body felt encased. For all intents and purposes she really could be at the bottom of her grave. *I soon will be if I don't get this off,* she thought.

The heat around her face rose in its intensity. She imagined her skin was blood red within the mask. This thing, whatever it was, would cook her brains. She pounded and scratched at the metal until the tips of her fingers stung. Lines of sweat streaked down her neck. The hysteria expanded like a balloon. She stepped off the bed and turned around and around, her fingers under the mask, yanking and pulling all the while, and all the while with no effect. Her frustration grew and increased her sense of terror. Spinning madly, she grew dizzy.

She screamed again and again, the sound of her voice deafening, and then she felt her body soften as if her bones had crumbled to dust within, and she sank to the floor, her heavy head bouncing hard on the rug. All went black.

When she woke again, she found herself on her back in the bed. She heard their voices before she saw them, but she didn't move.

"It would have been better if she were awake when you did it, Mommy. It doesn't come as such a shock then," Anna heard the man say.

"It was easier this way. It'll get used to it. The other incubators did. That wasn't what went wrong with them."

"I know."

"If it goes brain-dead, you'll just put it on an IV, Daddy. I'd rather it went brain-dead anyway. It's easier. Remember that pregnant woman who was in a coma at your hospital for seven months and they did a cesarean? The baby was perfect anyway, wasn't she?"

"Yes, she was. The woman died shortly afterward. It was as though her body knew it had to stay alive for the child," he said with wonder in his voice.

"It will be the same with this incubator here," she added.

Anna groaned. *Incubator?*

"It wakes," the woman said.

A moment later Anna saw the man lean over her, gazing into the socket holes like a medical examiner over a corpse. He smiled when he saw her eyes were open.

"Hello in there," he said.

"Take this off me, please," she begged.

"I can't do that if I wanted to. Mommy's the only one. She's the only one with the key, right, Mommy?"

"Right."

"Please. It's hot and very uncomfortable. I'll do whatever you want me to do. I promise."

"Oh, we know that," he said, smiling. "Don't we, Mommy?"

"It's not that hot in there," the woman said. She was standing just behind him. "I know how it feels. I tested it."

"She did," he said. "Can't lie to Mommy." His nostrils twitched. "She doesn't smell so good, Mommy. She smells like she peed in her pants. She smells like some of the old people in beds with the sides up."

"What's new about that?" the woman said. She pushed him aside and looked down at Anna. The woman's mouth writhed. "Get up. As long as you can stand, you'll change the bedding and your nightgown yourself and you'll bathe yourself, and if you don't, if you wallow in your own dirt and endanger the baby inside you, we'll tie you down and treat you like a total invalid. Understand?"

"Please," Anna begged. Her voice was thin and hoarse and her throat ached.

"Up!" the woman screamed. She pulled Anna's arm.

"Let me help," he said, taking the other arm. They forced her into a sitting position and then off the bed. She stood, but she wobbled.

The woman put her right forefinger between Anna's breasts and pressed hard, her fingernail like a small knife cutting into her skin, down to the bone.

"Stop trembling. Stop it!" She turned toward the dresser. "The second drawer has clean nightgowns and the third drawer has the clean sheets. Change the bedding and put the stained sheet at the door. Then take a bath and put on a new nightgown. Have it all done before we return with your supper. If it's not done, we'll consider you an invalid and treat you as such. Understand?" she threatened.

Anna tried to swallow but couldn't.

"Why?" she mouthed. She sucked in some air. "Why?" she said in a loud whisper.

"What?" the woman demanded, moving closer.

"Why did you do this?" she asked, her hands on the metal mask.

"Because I can't stand looking at you," the woman replied. "Now, do what you're told. Come on, Daddy. Let's get her supper ready. Remember what we told you. Remember to have it all done. And be careful when you take your bath. If you do anything to lose our baby . . ."

Anna shook her head.

"You'll never get this baby," she said, but she wasn't sure if she had said it or just thought it. The woman did not respond. However, he was at her side, his mouth close to the hole for her left ear.

"Don't get Mommy any more angry than she already is," he whispered as he walked by to join the woman at the door. He turned and smiled at her and then they left. She heard the lock being snapped shut.

Anna gazed around helplessly. *I've got to keep from cracking up completely,* she thought. *I've got to maintain control, otherwise I will never escape.* She realized that for the time being she had to be obedient, look cooperative, and keep them from being any more suspicious than they were. She took deep breaths, felt her heartbeat slow, and then began to rip off the soiled bedsheet.

After she had changed and made the bed, she ran the water for her bath. They had provided her with soap and bath oil and a washcloth. The towel was on the hamper beside the tub. Anna put in some bath oil, adjusted the water temperature, and watched the tub fill.

I won't eat anything tonight, she thought. *I'll dump it all down the toilet so they can't drug me to sleep, and tomorrow I'll wait for my opportunity and fight for my life. If I don't, I'll die here anyway,* she concluded. She had no doubt about that.

When there was sufficient water in the tub, she took off her nightgown and lowered herself into the bubbly bath. Taking a bath was actually a good idea. It soothed and calmed her. She lay back, closed her eyes, and for the moment forgot she was trapped and incarcerated in this mad place with these maddening people. Because immersing in the warm water provided Anna with some inner peace, albeit temporary, she couldn't help but recall the first time she had accompanied her mother to the *mikvah* for the ritual bath. Her mother had decided Anna was old enough to understand and appreciate the need for spiritual purification.

"You know married men and women have sexual relations often, Anna, and you know that we believe we should abstain from these relations when the woman is in *niddah* during her monthly menstruation period."

"Yes, Mama," she said. Her heart beat faster when she understood that her mother was going to speak to her on a woman-to-woman basis and not on a woman-to-child basis.

"Remember what the sages teach us, Anna: Strength comes from our ability to rule our passions and not allow our passions to master us. It is important to be able to abstain. You understand what I mean by *abstain?*"

"Yes, Mama," she said quickly, afraid her mother might stop talking about what used to be forbidden things.

"Just counting the days since her menstruation stopped doesn't remove a woman from her state of *niddah*, Anna, and permit her to resume her marital activity. We believe that requires a spiritual ritual, the immersion in a ritual bath, the *mikvah*. It's how we purify ourselves. Without it, a wife remains in her state of separation, forbidden to her husband, for it is written in Leviticus: 'You shall not come near a woman while she is impure by her uncleanness to uncover her nakedness.' "

"Why can't you just take a bath at home, Mama?"

Her mother laughed.

"It's not just a bath, Anna. In fact, all dirt must be scrupulously cleaned off our bodies before we go into the *mikvah*. Until a married woman immerses herself, she can't sleep in the same bed with her husband."

"Why is that, Mama?"

"They might forget themselves. That's why, as you know, we and other Orthodox religious couples have twin beds. The sexual urge is a powerful thing, Anna. We must respect that power and do what is necessary to control it. Otherwise, we can get into trouble, Anna. Remember this. The rituals, the beliefs, we cherish as a people have some root in logic, Anna."

Her body trembled in the tub as she recalled her mother's warning: "Remember this. . . ."

"Look where I am now, Mama. Look where I am."

She took deep breaths and then she recited the blessing a woman recited once she had immersed herself completely in the *mikvah*.

"*Baruch ata adonai elohainu melech ha-olam*

asher kidshanu b'mitzvotav v'tzivanu al hatvilah."

She closed her eyes and saw her mother standing there, preparing for her ritual bath, unfastening her beautiful long black hair and combing it out, a soft smile on her face.

The vision revived her.

"I will not die in this place, Mama."

She rose out of the water and stood with her arms folded under her breasts, her defiance growing.

"I will not die here."

She wiped herself dry and put on the clean nightgown. There was no mirror in the bathroom or the room, but she polished the pipe that brought the water to the tub and caught a bit of her reflection in the metal surface.

"My God," she muttered. As she had pictured with her hands, the mask was square. It was the same shade of white as the walls in the prison bedroom, and there were just the two holes for her nostrils, the holes for her eyes and her mouth. She turned and saw where the two sides of the mask were joined and she felt and made out the place where the key would be inserted to unlock it. There was no way to get it off without help. That would have to come after she accomplished her escape.

She returned to the bedroom and sat as calmly as she could, waiting. She had no idea of the time, of course, but she remembered the woman saying something about dinner. It wasn't long before she heard footsteps and then the key being inserted in the door. Anna had been hoping it would only be the woman, but they were both there.

The woman carried the tray. She paused and gazed down at the soiled sheet and nightgown on the floor near the door. She looked at the bed with its clean sheet.

"Well, well," the man said, coming up beside her. "Everything's in order, Mommy. She's behaving."

The woman said nothing. She brought the tray to the table and set it down. Anna was afraid they would stand over her and watch her eat as they had before. The woman went into the bathroom and saw Anna had bathed. She stared at the tub and once again Anna's heart raced. Would she see the scratches and dents in the bathtub faucet handle?

"You better eat before all this gets cold," the man said.

"How can I eat with this on my head?" she asked.

"Oh, you can fit everything in all right. You just have to eat slower is all, right, Mommy?"

"That's right. I know it can be done. I've done it. Eat and stop complaining."

Anna moved slowly to the chair. They hovered. She could pretend to be sick, to have an upset stomach, but they might just run out and bring in the intravenous bag as they had done the last time, and there was no telling what was in that solution.

More likely than not, there was a sedative of equal or greater strength.

She sat and began to eat.

"I'll get her dirty things, Mommy," the man said.

"Good." The woman stood there, her eyes small with suspicion and distrust. "My baby has to be healthy and strong," she said. "She has to have the best start a baby can have."

"It's not your baby," Anna said. She couldn't help it. She knew it would be better to remain quiet, but the outrage and anger had tightened her until she felt as though her whole body had become as hard as the metal of the mask.

She eyed the door as the man opened it, but he stood there, waiting with the linen and the nightgown in his arms.

"She'll eat it all, Mommy. She knows better than not to eat it all. Come on. We have more important things to do."

The woman looked at him and then at Anna. She picked up the glass of what looked like cranberry juice. It had a straw in it. She brought it to the mouth of the mask.

"Drink some of this," she ordered. Anna was sure that meant the sedative was in the juice.

She sucked on the straw as the woman held it, trying to take in as little as possible.

"Drink."

She took in more and tried to hold it in her mouth, rather than swallow, but the woman kept the glass up, so she had to swallow what she had.

"You don't have to feed her like a baby, Mommy," the man said. He smiled. "We have to think about our own dinner."

She put the glass down.

"When I return, I expect to see every morsel eaten," she said, and joined him at the door, where she again hesitated and watched Anna take her forkful of mashed potatoes.

"It's fine, Mommy. Everything is fine."

"Maybe," she said, looking back at Anna. "We'll see," she added, and followed him out.

The moment she heard the lock click and their footsteps start away, Anna got up and ran into the bathroom. She hovered over the toilet and put her fingers down her mouth to initiate regurgitation. It was messy getting it out of the opening for her mouth, but she did it. Much of what she had taken in came up, but it left her weak and tired. She sat on the floor and caught her breath. Then she returned to the table and brought the remaining food back to the bathroom. She flushed it all down the toilet and poured the juice in after it before placing the tray and dishes on the table again.

At least she would be alert in the morning. At least she would be ready to try some kind of escape. Anna hoped that only the woman would come in with her breakfast, as she had this morning.

Try to sleep, she told herself. *Try to conserve your strength, Anna Gold. You'll need it more than you ever needed it before.*

She closed her eyes. She could hear their footsteps above her and for a moment wondered if they had some sort of peephole and had been toying with her all this time, watching her work the chain loose from the wall, permitting her the illusion of the possibility of an escape.

There was no way to judge what they did, what they thought. They were beyond reason, operating on another plane, in a world of their own mad making. How did such people go undetected?

As she lay there she thought about her mother and the way her mother had accepted her final days. Her mother always worried about her father more than she worried about herself. Even then.

"He'll be in great pain, Anna. You and Miriam must be a comfort to him."

"You're the one in great pain, Mama."

"No. Where I'm going there is no more pain. I've accepted my fate."

I'm sick of acceptance, she thought. *We accept our horrible history of persecution; we accept the discrimination; we accept the bad luck, the sickness, and we accept death.*

I accept nothing.

No, Mama, no more. No, Papa, no more, even if it means risking your curses.

She thought she was going a little mad. She

thought she saw her father at the door with the two crazy people at his side.

"This is what comes of your defiance, Anna. I cannot help you now. All I can do is say Kaddish."

"No!" she screamed. *"You do not have to accept!"*

She sat up. There was no one at the door. All was quiet except for that rumbling on the other side of the wall, that monotonous grinding, cutting into her very soul.

She fell back on the bed and, as she had when she had first woken, imagined herself looking up from the bottom of her grave. She waited for the first spoonful of dirt and prayed it wouldn't be her father throwing it down on her coffin the day after her body had been found, empty, childless, discarded like a worthless, broken incubator.

19

Robert Royce was one of the new breed of lawyers who seemed to feed on deprecation. With an arrogant flair, he loved to pass on a new lawyer joke. He always followed it with "I'm laughing all the way to the bank."

In his mid-thirties, bright with those boyish good looks that took a man gently into his sixties and seventies, he swaggered with confidence through what he liked to call "the maze of justice." Few attorneys had his stage presence in court. He knew how to hold his trim six-foot-two-inch frame so as to exude strength and project to a jury or a judge. When opposing attorneys and members of juries first saw him with his shock of light brown hair lying over his forehead as if he had brushed it there with his fingers, and saw his twinkling, hazel brown eyes and soft, rich complexion, they were put off guard. They expected youth and inexperience, an "Aw, gee, I didn't know" to come out of that coy mouth.

But the moment he began, those images and expectations died a quick and painful death. He had a surprisingly deep, resonant voice that, if one heard it with his or her eyes closed, one would believe belonged to a man nearly twice his age. He was quick to see the point, quick to cut to the chase, quick to ridicule and cite precedent. Anyone who underestimated him paid dearly for it.

Most important, perhaps, was the fact that as one of the new breed of media-conscious lawyers, he knew how to use the camera and was a master of the sound bite. Unlike his older and more refined peers, he actively sought publicity and fed on it.

"If we've learned anything from the O.J. Simpson trial," he told his associates, "it's that legal battles are often won or lost in the headlines. And the same goes, therefore, for legal careers."

It was a simple axiom of modern times: A lawyer who was well known, no matter how that fame or notoriety was established, was a lawyer who could charge his clients more and yet was in more demand. To Robert Royce there was no such thing as bad publicity; there was just publicity.

And so it came as no surprise to those who knew him that he would decide to represent Roy Gault. Instead of the typical ambulance chaser, Robert Royce was the pursuer of fame, the king of sound bites. He held court on the steps of the courthouse, directing himself to the microphones above him as if he were speaking to the balcony in a theater, and then he fixed his sharp gaze on the camera lenses like one following the instruction of Orson Welles: Look as if you're looking into someone's face and make it seem personal.

"It's ridiculous to assume Mr. Gault left his home intending to commit murder," he declared after it was learned the district attorney was seeking to charge Gault with murder one. "How would he know Doctor Williams would come out and confront him and his followers directly? It was an act of utter rage, spontaneous, without malice aforethought."

"But Mr. Gault claims he was justified," one of the reporters shot back.

Robert Royce smiled.

"That's his religious belief. One man's fanatic is another man's messiah."

The cameras clicked. He had given the radio and television news reporters their opening remark and ensured himself of the top spot in the news intro: "One man's fanatic is another man's messiah."

Rightly assuming the case would attract statewide and national attention, Royce seized the opportunity and claimed this would be one of his pro bono cases, a matter of principle. Dr. Williams's death was horrible and should never have occurred, but America, he declared, was a land that prided itself on permitting diversity. The radical religious contingent had just as much right to exist as did the middle-of-the-road diehard Democratic and Republican organizations, traditional religious groups, and the Boy Scouts of America.

"I do not agree with what you say, but I will fight to the death for your right to say it," he offered with his disarmingly boyish smile.

In the back of his mind, he expected to plea-bargain Roy Gault into first-degree manslaughter. Yes, it was true that the case had everyone's interest and high exposure right now, but the machinations of the legal system would enable him to drag the proceedings through procedural hell, and after months and months it would lose its position on the front burner—which, he had concluded cynically years earlier, was when real justice and legal maneuvering finally took place in some judge's chambers.

For the moment, however, he was prone to milk it of every last drop of ink.

"The only reason Mr. Gault has been charged with first-degree murder is the district attorney's well-known ambition to run for Congress. However, I don't believe the public is that stupid," he concluded, even though everything he did was predicated on that very same assumption.

McShane stopped to buy a newspaper after leaving Cookie because he wanted to see if there was a picture of Robert Royce. There was a big one on the front page capturing Royce's courtroom-steps speech, his right arm in the air, his briefcase in his left hand, his gaze directed toward the heavens as if he were reciting a Shakespearean soliloquy. McShane quickly perused the news story and then headed for Royce's home. It was Sunday. Even the overwhelmingly ambitious took a day off.

McShane had learned that Robert Royce lived in a sprawling ranch-style home built on ten picturesque acres between Liberty and Neversink. The windows of the dining room looked out on the reservoir and the mountain range. The house itself had a rich red-brick finish and a front lawn as wide and as long as most homeowners' entire lots. The macadam driveway circled up to the front of the house and the three-car garage. There were ornamental pole lights with antique brass lanterns spaced along the way, and across the front lawn there were four small but richly green evergreens. Fall had dried up all the flowers and sent the leaves of surrounding hickory, beech, and maple trees tumbling in the wind, but the glittering late-afternoon sun made the well-manicured and maintained lawn look freshly grown and the windows and walkway sparkle.

When McShane drove up, he saw the garage door was opened and a late-model S-class silver Mercedes in the garage. The second space was empty and the third contained a golf cart. He hoped the empty space didn't mean Robert Royce wasn't home. When he stepped out of his car, he paused to gaze down at the reservoir. It looked near its full capacity, thanks to the late-summer storms. The water was silvery blue, peaceful, inviting. *What a wonderful spot for a home,* he thought. *A man could feel invulnerable up here.*

The front door had a circle of stained glass in the center. The door itself was built from rich dark oak. McShane pushed the door button and heard a tinkle of chimes tap out some familiar tune. As he waited for someone to come to the door, he tried to think of what it was. Robert Royce himself was soon there, dressed in a purple velvet smoking jacket and a pair of gray slacks. His hair was neatly brushed back on the sides with that trademark shock of some strands over his forehead. He looked as if he were preparing for a Barbara Walters interview.

"I've got a press conference first thing tomorrow morning at my office," he said quickly but with a smile. "Nine o'clock." He handed McShane a business card.

McShane took it but replied, "I'm not a reporter." He showed Royce his identification.

"Detective? Very interesting, but you know I can't talk about my client and the case, I'm sure."

"I'm not here about Roy Gault," McShane said. "At least, I don't know if I am."

"Don't know if you are? Well . . . you've got my attention, Detective"—he looked at McShane's card—"McShane. You have a good lead-in. How can I help you?" he asked, after folding his arms under his chest. It was apparent he had no intention of inviting McShane into the house.

"Do you know an Anna Gold?"

Royce blinked and his right eyebrow lifted with the twist in the right corner of his mouth.

"That depends on why you're asking," he said.

"I don't see how your knowing or not knowing her would depend on that," McShane countered. Royce just stared. "I found your cellular phone number in her Rolodex when I searched her apartment."

Royce's face softened.

"She's a client—or, I should say, a potential client—of mine," he offered. "Why are you asking me about her? Why did you search her apartment?"

"Her story will be in tomorrow's paper. She was apparently abducted while in the Van's parking lot."

"What?" Royce grimaced. " 'Abducted'? What the hell's that mean?"

"Someone's kidnapped her. The FBI is involved in this too," McShane added, hoping that would win him a more cooperative Robert Royce.

"Really?" He shook his head. "I'm sorry to hear this."

"What did you mean when you said 'potential client'?"

Royce shook his head again, this time more emphatically.

"I'm afraid anything more comes under the attorney-client privilege, Detective. I will tell you that it's been nearly a week since I last spoke with her."

"Why would she have your cellular number?"

Royce shook his head.

"Look," McShane said, "this is a young woman who has literally disappeared. She is probably in great danger. I'm not trying to overly dramatize the situation, but the FBI has reason to believe she might be a victim of something very sinister. Whatever you tell me will be off the record. I can assure you of that."

"Where's the FBI?" Royce asked suspiciously.

"I'm handling this aspect."

Royce considered.

"All right. Come on in," he said, and stepped back.

McShane entered and Royce closed the door. He indicated a room to the right, which was an office furnished with two red leather settees, a red leather cherry-wood chair, a large cherry-wood desk and swivel chair, and matching coffee and side tables. The wall to the left was a built-in bookcase filled with volumes of classic literary works as well as modern novels and nonfiction books. There were two large panel windows behind the desk. The dark brown drapes were pulled back so the woods were in full view. On the right wall Royce had hung his award plaques and some pictures of himself with a variety of celebrities on the local golf courses; there were also pictures of him with a woman whom McShane assumed was his wife. She was an attractive woman but looked a bit dour in all the pictures. McShane noted that there were no pictures of children.

"Have a seat," Royce said, indicating the settee on the left. McShane sat and Royce went to the chair. He crossed his legs and folded his hands in his lap. "I don't know if you know it," he began, "I don't know who she told, if anyone, but Anna Gold is pregnant."

"I'm aware of that. As far as I know now, this early in the investigation, only her sister knew—and, from what her sister told me, her lover."

Royce nodded.

"Lover," he said with a sneer.

"Do you know who he is?" McShane asked.

Royce shook his head.

"Anna Gold is a very naive and innocent young woman. She's more like a teenager because she was so cloistered all of her life. As you know if you spoke to her sister, Anna comes from an Orthodox Jewish family. She's sweet but vulnerable. Whoever this cad is, she fell for him hook, line, and sinker, as they say. She believes his promises, but she was beginning to experience some doubt, and that was why she came to see me."

"If she wanted you to go after him, she must have told you his name."

"That wasn't it," Royce said, shaking his head and smiling. "This type of woman, emotionally and socially undeveloped, usually never goes after the man." He spoke as if he were a man of age and wisdom. His confident, self-assured air annoyed McShane, but he nodded and listened politely. "I've had my share of divorce cases and know whereof I speak," he added.

"I bet."

"No, Anna wouldn't give me a name. She wanted to protect the creep. She blamed herself for the predicament she was in. The last time I spoke with her, she even intimated it might have something to do with an angry God taking retribution." He shook his head. "We are surrounded by wackos of all sorts and shapes wrapping themselves in one religious banner or another."

He paused as if he were constructing his next sound bite.

"I still don't follow you. Why did you say she was a potential client, then?" McShane asked.

Royce stared a moment and then sat back, placing his hands on the arms of the chair.

"One of the things I do, which is pretty lucrative for me, is arrange for legal adoptions. Anna, who works in the public defender's office, as you undoubtedly know, came into contact with a pregnant woman who was being defended for repeated shoplifting. The woman told her what she was going to do about her pregnancy, which had gone too far. I think she was just too stupid to think about an abortion, myself. Anyway, soon afterward, Anna came to see me to find out about the option. This is why I said she was having some doubts about her lover boy and his promises."

"You were going to set up an adoption of her child?"

"I have it in the works if she wants it. She was supposed to tell me this coming week. The couple is very anxious about it. They are willing to take care of all of Anna's living expenses, put her up in their guest house until she gives birth."

"Why give her your cellular number?"

"I gave her all my numbers, even my unlisted home number. As I said, this couple is very anxious. They were pleased to hear about Anna's condition and what sort of a person she was. They thought the baby was perfect for them and"—he paused and leaned forward—"they added some financial incentive to my fee. I, er . . . have the highest respect for added financial incentives," he said, smiling.

"Anna was very much on the fence about it," he continued, sitting back again. "I thought if she calls and says she wants to go ahead with the adoption, I had better jump on it and get it arranged quickly. So I gave her all my numbers."

McShane nodded.

"I don't want to see any of this in some news story," Royce warned.

"You won't."

"You don't have any leads, then, as to the man involved?"

"Not really. I think one of her girlfriends might know. She was reluctant to tell me. Some woman-to-woman loyalty thing, but I think I'll get her to tell me all she knows the next time I interview her," he said confidently.

"Let me know if there is anything I can do to help. I'm fairly successful when it comes to per-suading women," he said, smiling.

"Really? I'm not," McShane said, and thought a moment. "Tell me more about this couple."

"I never saw two people more desperate to have a child. I think they were considering a trip to Romania, only they're not keen on foreign children, nor do they travel much. They're not all that wealthy—some family money."

"Can you give me their names?"

"Oh, absolutely not. I couldn't do that. That would really be a breach of ethics."

"Do you think there's any possibility they were desperate and impatient enough to move things along?" McShane asked.

"You mean kidnap her?" Royce thought a moment. "I doubt it, but who can swear about any-one these days?"

"The FBI thinks this might be tied into the radi-cal religious right, the antiabortion movement."

"Why?"

"Anna also took a look at another option."

"Abortion?"

"Apparently she visited the clinic."

Royce stared and then blew through his closed lips. His eyes brightened.

"You mean something similar has happened someplace else, then? Is that why the FBI is so interested?"

"Has to be off the record," McShane said.

"Quid pro quo."

"Yes, apparently so. So," he continued, "you can see why it's important for me to determine if this is part of it all or an isolated incident. I'd just like to look over this couple, maybe observe them, just to see."

"If they have Anna Gold locked up someplace?"

"Got to do something," McShane said.

Royce thought.

"It's going to be hard observing them. They live kind of out of the way."

"I'm a former successful Peeping Tom."

Royce laughed. He thought and then he stood up.

"I'm going to write down the name of a street, put down a couple of X's, and circle one which indicates a residence. I'm relying on you being discreet."

"Good enough."

"Of course, I'd like to be kept informed."

"Quid pro quo. You've got my card. If anything comes to mind or you hear anything . . ."

Royce nodded and went to his desk. He wrote and drew on a slip of paper and then he handed it to McShane, who stood up.

"Thanks."

"I'm kind of caught in between two hopes," Royce said as he escorted him to the door. "That you don't find anything suspicious, and yet, you do find Anna Gold."

"I understand."

After Royce opened the door and McShane stepped out, he said, "One more thing."

"Yes?"

"If anything suspicious involving my clients proves true, I want the opportunity to make a statement to the press before the district attorney gets his face in the papers."

"My first concern is Anna Gold," McShane said dryly.

"Of course. It's mine too," Royce replied, smiled, and then closed the door.

McShane gazed at the slip of paper in his hand and then hurried to his car to pursue what he felt might very well be the solution to the case.

Won't Cookie be proud of me? he thought.

But it won't bring her back, his alter ego pointed out.

20

She had taken great pains to make their dinner special. She was a good cook, a very good cook. Growing up in a home where love was rarely expressed and especially very rarely expressed to her, she felt like Cinderella before the prince had arrived with the glass slipper. Even though her sister was older, her mother made her help in the kitchen and insisted that she learn how to prepare food.

"It's probably the only way you'll win a man," her mother told her. Her sister was prettier in those days, with a voluptuous figure, whereas she always had a more masculine, tomboy look.

Ironically, this discrimination only made her into a better, more capable and independent person, unlike her sister, who had to have someone cook for her and her husband, clean their home, and care for their children. Her sister was truly an invalid now, she thought, stricken down by laziness, indolent, and slothful. She had become fat and spoiled and was a blob with a mouth. And her brother wasn't much better, with his spoiled wife and undisciplined pack of rug rats. Good riddance to them, she thought, time and time again.

She didn't need them. She had Daddy, and soon she and Daddy would have a family of their own. Finally.

She stood to the side in the dining room and surveyed her work. The table absolutely glittered. Their best china was set out with their best silverware and goblets. The candles burned and she had dressed the table in one of her prettiest tablecloths and matching napkins. Daddy put on romantic music, a Henry Mancini album. He had changed into a jacket, tie, and slacks and she wore one of her nicest dresses, her most expensive earrings with the tiny rubies in the middle, and its matching necklace. Daddy had shaved closely; she had sprayed herself with her most expensive perfume. It was meant to be one of those evenings they would never forget.

And it started out that way too. Daddy opened the wine and poured her a glass and then one for himself. They made a toast, followed with a kiss, and then they drank. She brought out the salad with the hot, fresh bread she had baked herself. Daddy complimented everything. He couldn't say enough. She laughed, she held his hand, they conversed as they had not conversed in ages. Daddy told her about his day at work and the things he had overheard and seen. He made sure to tell her about Tommy Patterson's remark. She beamed, a lighthouse in a world whose nights were usually without stars.

"What a nice thing for him to say."

"Everyone at work wishes us well," Daddy told her.

It put tears in her eyes. Strangers wishing them well. How wonderful and how ironic that strangers would care for them more than the members of their own families. She dabbed at her eyes with the cloth napkin and rose to bring out the duck.

"Can I help?"

"No, just sit and enjoy, Daddy," she said. "I'll be the cook, waitress, and chief bottle washer tonight." He smiled and she went into the kitchen.

But before she could return, the phone rang.

She stared at it for a moment, as if she knew who was calling. It rang again.

Daddy was in the doorway.

"You want me to get it?" he asked. She nodded and turned to put the duck on the platter, her fingers trembling nervously in expectation.

"Hello," Daddy said. When he listened so long without saying anything, it compounded her fears. What was wrong?

Daddy had his back to her and was nodding as if the caller could see.

Finally he said, "I understand. I'll take care of it immediately. Yes, I'm on my way."

He replaced the receiver and stood there with his back to her for a moment, gathering his thoughts.

"What?" she demanded.

"Someone is trying very hard to take our baby away from us," he told her.

She brought her hand to her mouth and sucked in her worst fears.

"It's a policeman and he has found someone who might tell him things that eventually would bring him here. I'm sorry," he said, looking at the duck on the platter. "I've got to go. It's for the baby," he added.

Of course she understood.

"Go, Daddy. Do what you have to do."

He nodded and went up to their bedroom. He didn't change out of his good clothes; he went to the closet and reached up for the medical bag on the shelf. After he checked to be sure all he needed was inside, he closed it and descended the stairs. She was waiting at the bottom, wringing her hands, her face full of worry.

"Is that the best way?" she asked, nodding at the bag.

"Yes," he said. "No mess, no fuss, no one comes knocking on our front door."

"Do you want me to go with you?"

"Oh, no, Mommy. No. You stay and finish your dinner."

"I can't eat without you," she snapped. "It'll wait."

He nodded.

"I'll be back as soon as I can," he told her, and kissed her cheek.

She watched him leave and then she turned and walked furiously to the kitchen to put everything else on hold. Why? She wondered, stomping her feet, why was it so easy for other people? Why was it so easy for her blob of a sister? She pounded her fists against her thighs so hard in frustration, she felt pain, but she didn't stop. She pounded again and again until she grew exhausted and sat at the kitchen table. Tears streaked down her face.

"We're not going to lose this baby. We're not!" she said. She gazed at the clock. She wouldn't move. She'd wait right here for Daddy's successful return.

He jerked the car back so hard and accelerated so abruptly in the driveway, the wheels spit the gravel behind him, some stones actually hitting the house. He bounced down the back road, knowing he was driving too fast, but he couldn't help it. He so wanted this to be a good night for Mommy, and for himself. They deserved it. They had earned it!

It was all supposed to go so perfectly; it was all supposed to be so simple.

When he turned onto the main road, he pulled out without looking and nearly collided with an oncoming vehicle turning into their road. The driver leaned on his horn and it blared into the night behind him, but he didn't slow down until he reached the first traffic light and got ahold of himself. He realized he didn't want to attract any undue attention. The remainder of the journey, therefore, was uneventful.

He eased into her parking lot less than a half hour later and waited a moment to be sure no one would see him arrive. Then he reached for his bag, unzipped it, and quickly filled the syringe so it would be ready. When that was done, he got out of the car, keeping as deeply in the shadows created by the parking-lot lights and the lights around the complex as he could until he was at her door. He stood there, gazing around.

It was deadly quiet, with no signs of anyone. Above him the sky was as dark as the beginning of a nightmare. A thick overcast shut out the half-moon and stars. That was fine with him.

He opened the bag and quickly put on the surgical gloves. Then he took out the syringe and clutched it like a dagger in his right hand. He took a deep breath to gather his courage and resolve, remembering the words of hope and encouragement between Mommy and him. Finally he pushed the door buzzer sharply, quickly, and dropped his right hand behind his leg so the syringe would be out of sight.

Moments later, her Taser in hand, Lidia

Ambrook opened the door enough to peer out. The hand holding the Taser was behind the door.

"Yes?"

He was a nicely dressed man. The tension in her chest eased a bit.

"Lidia Ambrook?"

"Yes."

"Thank God," he said. "Anna Gold sent me."

"Anna? Where is she?"

"She's in trouble. She needs your help," he said. "May I come in a moment?"

She considered and then opened the door wider and he entered, spinning around as he did so as to shut the door with his bag and simultaneously drive the needle into the soft area at the base of her skull. It took her by surprise, but she raised her Taser and attempted to point it at him. He dropped the bag and grabbed her right wrist with his left hand, keeping the needle embedded, the plunger down, as he held the Taser away from him. She tried to kick him between the legs, but he antici- pated that and, using his body, drove her back against the door. He slammed her right hand against the wood at the same time and the Taser fell to the floor.

She finally found the strength to scream, so he released her right wrist and put his wrist, cuff and all, into her mouth, pressing as he did so. She pushed desperately at his chest, but he held her there, pinning her right side against the door and continuing to empty the syringe. She tried to get her hands free to pound him with her small fists, but he was all over her, his body keeping her left hand down, her right hand not getting back enough to deliver any sort of blow.

Her eyes fluttered. He felt her resistance dwindling. Her face was full of panic, but when her eyeballs went back, the panic seemed to evaporate and be replaced with an empty, restful expression. He smiled. It was almost over. Her body began to sink as her legs gave way. He let her slide down the door to the carpet, where he turned her over on her stomach and removed the needle.

He opened the bag and took out a cotton swab, which he used to wipe away the drop of blood at the base of her neck. He cleaned the tiny wound until it was undetectable by the human eye. He dropped the swab into his bag and closed it, stood up, and gazed down at her.

Her body shuddered and then grew still. He waited and then knelt down and felt for a pulse. Satisfied, he opened the door and peered out. Seeing or hearing no one, he closed the door softly behind him, slipped back into the shadows, and wove his way to his car. He got in quietly and returned the syringe to the bag, along with the gloves. Then he started the engine and backed out with his headlights off until he reached the entrance to the parking lot.

It took all his self-control to drive home at a reasonable speed. He was so anxious to tell Mommy that all would be well again. She was just where he had left her: in the kitchen. When he entered, she looked up expectantly. He smiled.

"That's that," he said. "All finished."

"It went all right?"

"Perfect, Mommy. Baby's safe again." His smile widened, so she relaxed.

"Thank God," she said, and stood. She looked at the duck. "Oh, I'll have to warm that."

"Go on. I'll just put this back," he said, holding up the bag, "and throw some cold water on my face. I worked up a little sweat."

She nodded.

"You're a good Daddy."

He smiled again and went upstairs. Minutes later he returned and they were at their dinner again as if nothing at all had happened, except he had worked up a bigger appetite.

"This is so good," he said, munching on the pieces of duck. "Succulent and not greasy. How do you do it, Mommy?"

"Family trade secrets," she replied, and he laughed. "Which I will pass on to my daughter," she said firmly.

"That's right. Just think of all that you can give our children."

"That's all I *do* think about, Daddy."

He nodded sympathetically, his eyes closing.

"I know. Soon enough, eh?"

"Not soon enough. I wish there was a way to speed up the incubation."

"There isn't, Mommy. Those doctors who try those drugs to make things happen faster usually regret it," he added with a scowl.

She nodded.

"I realize I'm impatient," she admitted.

"You've waited a long time. No one can blame you, Mommy," he said, reaching across the table to put his hand gently over hers.

She smiled at him. Such understanding.

"Wait until you see our dessert," she said, and went to fetch it. She returned with the strawberry shortcake and his mouth watered. "And there's French roast too."

She brought out the silver coffeepot and cut the cake. They both moaned with delight as they finished their feast.

"I'll help you clean up," he said. She looked at him askance.

"I think I know why you're in such a rush," she said teasingly. He blushed but continued to gather the dishes.

After everything was rinsed off and put in the dishwasher and the tablecloth and napkins were thrown in the washing machine, Mommy yawned and stretched.

"I think I'm tired," she said. "I think I'll go up to bed."

He looked disappointed and she laughed.

"Poor Daddy. Why don't you go up first," she said, and he smiled. He hurried away and up the stairs. She straightened a few more things in the kitchen and waited what she felt was enough time. Then she took the bottle of skin oil out of the bag on the counter where Daddy had left it, and she started up the stairs. "I'm coming," she sang.

She paused in the bedroom doorway.

There was Daddy lying in bed, naked, his hands behind his head, his pendulum just a trifle raised in expectation.

"Time for your reward," she said. His smile widened as she drew closer. She put the bottle of skin oil on the bed and slowly took off her dress. Daddy's smile froze and then evaporated. She was always intrigued by the changes in his face just before she did this. His eyes grew smaller; his mouth became tight and serious. It was almost as if a different man hovered inside him, just waiting for this opportunity to emerge.

Once, when she was not quite nine, her brother, who was fourteen, came down to the basement without realizing she was sitting in the far right dark corner, one of her private places. He had one of those forbidden girlie magazines inside his shirt. He sat near the basement window to get the light and took out the magazine. As he turned the pages he unzipped his fly and began to fondle himself. She watched, intrigued, fascinated, and nearly cried out when she saw him ejaculate. As soon as he had he closed himself up and left the basement. She waited, her heart pounding, and then she crossed to where he had been sitting and gazed down at the white blobs. She couldn't help but touch one and then smell it.

This was where babies began? How could this be? She broke a tiny sliver of wood from a crate and scooped some of the sticky wetness. She kept it for days and watched it dry, expecting to see some suggestion of life. But there was nothing, a big disappointment. That tape they had shown in school was just a cartoon after all.

Of course, she learned better, and in time she understood, but she never got the opportunity to experience the mystery of life within herself. For her it all remained a fantasy, something magical that happened to other people but not to her— never to her.

But why should Daddy suffer because of that? she thought. He was loyal; he was loving.

She poured the oil into her palm and rubbed her hands and then she moved over him.

It was the best way she knew to say thank you, especially after what he had just done and what he would continue to do.

21

McShane sat back in the front seat of his car. It had taken him a lot longer than he had anticipated to find this street and the house indicated by Robert Royce's circled *X*. There were so many new side roads in the area where people had built second bedroom homes or summer residences. He had actually driven by this road before realizing it was there. He turned back, found it, and followed the primitive sketch.

When he located the house, he parked just off the left shoulder of the road, backing up under an old, sprawling maple. But there was no need to look for a shadowy spot. Night fell much earlier these days. The heavy overcast and the absence of streetlights put the road and its surroundings into a sea of ink. From this location he could observe the house undetected. There were lights on downstairs, and from time to time he saw the silhouette of someone moving about, but there was little or no activity outside the house. It was really too dark to tell, but it looked as though the house were on a nicely maintained piece of property with some small structure in the rear. To the right of the house, a giant weeping willow tree loomed. McShane always thought weeping willows looked sad, like someone with his or her head down, the falling tears frozen in midair.

He was about to get out and reconnoiter when a shaft of light came down the road, indicating an approaching vehicle. He slid down in his seat as far as he could and waited, expecting it to pass.

But the car appeared and then turned into the driveway. A man stepped out and hurried to the front door, apparently not noticing him or his car across the way. It was hard to read details about the driver, but he appeared tall, lean, and well dressed. He went inside quickly and all was quiet again. McShane waited, watched the lit windows, and decided he had to risk getting closer. Anna Gold could very well be held prisoner in this house.

But just as he opened the door to step out, his beeper went off. He shut it quickly and backed in again. Then he reached for his radio phone and called the station.

"I hope I'm not interrupting your dinner," Marta said. "But . . ."

"What's up?"

"Sheriff wanted me to call you and get you on an unattended death. Medical examiner is already there."

"What do we have?"

"Twenty-five-year-old woman discovered by her mother."

"Where?"

"Just inside the front door, expired on the floor."

"What's the address?" She told him and he felt the heat come into his face with the recognition. "What's the name of the dead woman?"

"Lidia Ambrook," Marta said.

He blew out the air that had been heated in his lungs and started the car. As he pulled away he gazed at the house again, frustrated, but shot with a new rush of adrenaline. As soon as he got back on the main highway, he slapped on his bubble light and punched the accelerator.

When he arrived at Lidia Ambrook's apartment complex, he saw the coroner's car parked beside Leo Hallmark's patrol vehicle. Leo stood just outside the doorway with a small crowd of curious area residents nearby.

"What do we have, Leo?" he asked, approaching.

"I don't know. Ted Davis is in there trying to figure that out. I had Gerry take the mother over to some friends."

"Stabbed, shot, what?"

"Nothing violent as far as I could see from the door," Hallmark said.

McShane looked into the apartment. Teddy Davis, the medical examiner, was bagging Lidia Ambrook's hands. The forty-year-old pathologist looked up, his bushy eyebrows lifting as he shook his head with a wry smile.

"What d'ya have?"

"Twenty-five-year-old Caucasian female, deceased."

"I know that. I know her."

"Really? Know her well?"

"No. I interviewed her yesterday concerning a friend of hers who's missing."

"I see."

"What did it? Anything obvious?"

"No," he said, still with that wry smile. "Nothing obvious."

"So why are you bagging her hands?"

Teddy Davis stopped smiling.

"See that?" He pointed to the Taser.

"Yeah, it's a Taser. She was a little paranoid and had it with her whenever she came to her door. As I said, I interviewed this woman yesterday, so I know," McShane told him.

"Oh, you know?" Davis grinned again. "Come on down," he said, and McShane stepped over Lidia's legs and knelt beside him. It was hard looking into the dead face of a young woman he had just met. The death of someone this young was especially difficult to accept. Oddly, it was always easier to confront it when it was murder. That was explainable.

Teddy put his forceps into Lidia Ambrook's gaping mouth. Her eyes were bulged, her lips were blue, and her swollen tongue was a sickly pink. He lifted the tongue.

"See the trauma under here? Sometimes heart attack victims bite down on their own tongues, but this is different."

"I don't understand," McShane said. He was glad he hadn't eaten yet.

"No trauma on top of the tongue. She didn't bite down. This tongue was pressed down on the lower teeth very hard. See?" Teddy pointed out the trauma with his gloved finger.

McShane nodded.

"That got me wondering. I spoke to her mother before she was taken off. She said the girl has no history of heart disease. No problem with any vital organs."

"Any other sign of violence?" McShane asked impatiently.

"Yeah, I think so. Look up here," Davis replied, standing. He stepped carefully over Lidia Ambrook's corpse and pointed to the door. "She died right here, so I checked around a bit after I found that tongue trauma."

He pulled a small magnifying glass from his top pocket and handed it to McShane. Then he pointed to a spot on the door. "What d'ya see?"

McShane looked.

"Nothing?"

"Look closely, Detective. See the strand of hair embedded?"

"Yeah," McShane said. "I do."

"It looks like it matches hers. Someone held this woman's head against this door hard enough while she struggled against him to leave a strand embedded in the paint." Davis circled the spot and then carefully extracted the strand and placed it in a plastic bag. "I checked her scalp. It's red over here," he said, indicating the right side of Lidia Ambrook's cranium.

"You think she might have been strangled?"

"No trauma around her throat."

"Something could have been thrown over her head—a plastic bag."

"Yeah, but then how do you explain the hair on the door?"

"Right," McShane said.

"There's no trauma I could find with a precursory examination indicating she was beaten. We'll have to wait for a full autopsy, but I have no doubt the struggle was right here and it was quick and efficient. Something was put in her mouth to keep her from screaming."

"So how was she killed? No knife wound, no gun wound, no trauma around her neck. She wasn't strangled. Poison?" McShane asked.

"Have to wait for the autopsy for a full report, but . . ."

"But?"

"Ingested poison takes a while, and you got to force her to swallow. So . . ."

"So?"

Davis raised his eyebrows again. The intensity with which the man enjoyed his ghoulish work disturbed McShane, but he didn't want to appear queasy or unappreciative. Obviously, Davis saw himself as an artist of some sort.

"Injection," he said. "Recently, I had that elderly lady over in Mountaindale, remember? Her stepson injected her with nitro to bring on the heart attack, but I didn't find that until we were in the lab. I was luckier here because this woman does have one tiny little health problem."

"Really? What?"

"Whoever did this didn't know the woman suffered from a rare form of hemophilia. I checked with the mother. It was under control, but she had episodes, and apparently, after the killer cleaned the wound, he didn't hang around to check it."

He turned her head slightly and showed McShane the small trauma on the back of her neck.

"If you hold my magnifying glass over this, you'll see the pinprick."

"Jesus."

"We'll do a toxicology immediately. My guess, it's some kind of neural anesthetic, which would explain why she appears to have suffocated. We'll see.

"In any case," Davis concluded, "this is a murder

scene and we had better start treating it as such."

"Right," McShane said. He gazed at Lidia Ambrook's corpse again and recalled her fear about going out alone, and her belief in astrology. Apparently her paranoia was justified and her ability to predict for herself was very limited.

After McShane made sure the area was taped off, he questioned some of the residents, hoping one might have seen something. No one had.

"I just heard her mother screaming," a brunette no more than twenty-five herself told him. "That's when I came out. Was it another attack? Someone was nearly raped here two weeks ago."

"We haven't fully investigated yet, but it doesn't appear to be a sex thing. Did you know her well?"

"No," she said backing away as if he were going to ask her to do something more. "We just said hello."

The obvious question in his mind was: Was this murder unrelated or in some way connected to Anna Gold's abduction? He went to where Lidia Ambrook's mother had gone, a friend's home about two miles away, but her doctor had already put her under sedation. His questions would have to wait until morning, so he returned to the station to report to Ralph Cutler, who sat calmly listening to McShane's summary of what Teddy Davis had told him. The state bureau of criminal investigation had already dispatched a forensic man to the scene.

"A doctor is killed in the middle of an anti-abortion protest, a young woman is abducted, and another young woman is murdered? All in this county and all within forty-eight hours? When I first started here, violent death was something you saw only during big-game season." He shook his head. "All right. Give those forgeries to Billy to handle and dig into this new situation."

"They may be related," McShane said.

Cutler's eyes widened. "What may be related?"

"The abduction and this murder."

McShane reminded him who Lidia Ambrook was.

Cutler brightened. "Maybe we can get the FBI to take this on too, then."

"Doesn't fit into their MO, does it?"

"That's for them to decide. I'll pass it on to Reynolds and see what he says."

"In the meantime I'd better stay on it in case they conclude it's got nothing to do with their conspiracy theory, huh?" McShane fished.

"Absolutely. Keep me informed, Jimmy. Don't forget to give Billy the material on the forgeries."

"Oh, I won't forget that, Sheriff," McShane said.

Cutler laughed. "Whatever happened to the guy always looking for the easy way out?"

McShane thought a moment and then smiled. "I don't know, Sheriff, but next time I see him, I'll tell him you asked for him."

Ralph Cutler's laughter resounded behind him

as he left the office and headed back to Lidia Ambrook's to see if the state's forensic man had come up with anything new. Because of the lateness of the hour, the curious neighbors had gone to the safety and security of their own apartments, most not yet knowing this was a murder in their midst. Lidia's body had been removed and a chalk circle drawn around the area in which she had lain.

The forensic detective, a young Vietnamese man, was dusting the door for prints when McShane arrived. He was wearing gloves and booties. McShane introduced himself quickly.

"You walked in here before?" the criminalist asked quickly.

"Yeah, I came in when Ted Davis, the medical examiner, was checking her out and—"

"Those the shoes you wore?" he said, nodding at McShane's feet.

"Huh? Yeah, why?"

"Take them off, please," he ordered. "You shouldn't have walked in here."

McShane slipped off his shoes and the forensic detective took them and turned them over. He studied the soles and then he went to his case and took out some high-powered magnifying lenses. After he gazed through them a moment, he shook his head.

"Can't be sure you didn't bring it in, but I found shale in the carpet right here," he said, indicating the area near the circle. "Can't find any anywhere else in the place. Good chance the killer had shale on his shoes."

"Shale?"

"Yeah, it's used a lot in driveways around here where people don't blacktop."

"Oh. Anything else?"

"Nothing earthshaking," he said, and handed McShane his shoes. "Don't you guys review what to do and what not to do at a crime scene?" he asked.

"Sure, but—"

"You'd think, after watching the O.J. hearings, every cop would be on his toes."

"I didn't watch them," McShane said dryly. "They conflicted with *One Life to Live.*"

The criminalist raised his left eyebrow.

"If you want to come back in here, put on those booties for now," he said, indicating another pair near the door. He resumed dusting for prints.

McShane slipped the booties over his feet and entered the apartment. He recalled that it was a neatly arranged apartment, clean and orderly yet much warmer than Anna Gold's. This had the feel of someone living here. He searched the drawers in the kitchen, checked every slip of paper he found, every note on the counter. Most were reminders of one sort or another. There were some recipes, titles of books or records she was supposed to get, but nothing with Anna's name on it.

He went into the bedroom.

The bed was still made and, like the rest of the apartment, not a thing was out of place. The chances were great that she hadn't been entertaining her assailant. The attack had to have been immediate, probably as soon as he had come through that front door.

But why did she let him in? he wondered as he gazed at a silver-framed college graduation picture of Lidia Ambrook and an older couple who were surely her parents. Knowing how fearful she was, he assumed she either had known the assailant or he had said something to keep her from hitting him with the Taser the moment he came into the apartment.

He went through her night tables, checked the closet, even explored the pockets of some jackets, but found nothing interesting. He was hoping for a note, a letter, something that might lead him to Anna Gold's lover. He felt confident now that Lidia Ambrook had known who he was.

Frustrated, he left the bedroom and returned to the kitchen. Then he paused in the doorway of the dining room. There was something on the table, some papers. Sifting through them, he realized that Lidia Ambrook had been doing astrological charts for people. There was one for Anna Gold. The conclusions Lidia had described the day before were scribbled on the page. But under Anna Gold's chart was another that simply read *Anna's* with three dots following. One of the conclusions at the bottom put a chill in him, for whomever this chart belonged to was, like him, a Scorpio. This person's birthday was October 29. The conclusion read: *Be careful about radical decisions. Most will have long-term negative effects.*

He folded the paper and put it in his pocket.

A fortune-teller who could predict for everyone but herself, he thought.

Ironies were raining down and bouncing around him like hail.

He left to ponder what he knew.

22

Even though she believed she had regurgitated most of what she thought to be a sedative, Anna had trouble staying awake. So confined in this small room, she had done very little that required physical effort, but the emotional and mental strain was great. Operating continuously at the height of tension, her nerves were frayed and her heart pounded with trepidation over what would occur next. As a result, she experienced a fatigue that seemed to emanate from deep within her and radiate out through her arms and legs, up her neck, and into her very brain. It got so she couldn't think.

The metal square that had been locked around her head and her face intimidated her anyway. She kept her eyes closed most of the time so she wouldn't confront the encasement. It put an ache in her throat and made it difficult for her to swallow, even to breathe. It was better to sleep and wait for her opportunity to get free, an opportunity she knew she must have soon in order to survive mentally.

The constant whirring and grinding from the other side of the wall worked as an anesthetic again. She drifted and fell into a shallow repose— shallow because the moment she heard the sound of the key being inserted into the door lock, her eyes snapped open. She listened keenly and heard what she recognized as the woman's footsteps, for the woman walked with an almost military sharpness.

From the sound of it, the woman went directly to the tray and dishes to inspect how Anna had eaten. She stood there for a few moments. Anna didn't move a muscle. She even controlled her breathing so she would appear to be asleep. If the woman saw that she was awake, she might suspect that Anna had dumped the food, which included the sedative, down the toilet. Then there might be more hell to pay.

Minutes seemed to roll by without a sound, without the woman taking another step. Anna had the sensation she was being studied. She kept her eyes closed and she prayed. Finally the woman stepped up to the bed. Anna could hear her quickened breathing, the inhaling and exhaling through her open mouth. She braced herself for whatever the woman might do.

I must not move, she told herself. *I must not jump, even reflexively.*

It was a wise strategy, for moments later she felt the woman's hand on her stomach. She stood there with her palm over Anna's belly for what seemed, again, like minutes but was probably only seconds. Then Anna heard a deep sigh and felt the woman seat herself on the mattress. She thought she heard her whimper.

The woman's hand moved gently over Anna's belly and down her thigh, where it took hold of the nightgown and began to lift it up until most of Anna's abdomen was uncovered. The woman put her palm there again.

Suddenly she began to hum what sounded like an old lullaby. Anna felt her rocking on the bed, but she kept her eyes tightly shut, her breathing as regular as she could, even though her heart had begun to pound. She perceived the woman moving on the bed, lowering herself until the woman's lips touched her stomach.

"My little one," she said, kissing Anna's stomach softly. "My poor little one. I know you just hate it in there, hate being locked up in a place you're not wanted, but it won't be long before you're out and with me and never again where you are not wanted.

"I hope you're a girl," she continued. She kept her mouth only an inch or so from Anna's belly while she spoke. "As soon as you're old enough, you'll work beside me in the kitchen and we'll take walks together and talk about nature. There's a lot I have to tell you and show you.

"But I won't hog you. Daddy has a lot to tell you and show you too. Daddy's a good man, full of love. I suppose he wants you to be a boy, but don't worry, because it won't be long before you'll have a brother and maybe a sister. They'll be close to you too. They won't be like my brother and sister are to me, strangers with the same blood. You won't need them; you won't need such an uncle and aunt. We'll be enough family for you.

"So grow, my precious, grow as fast as you can. As soon as you're ready, I promise, I'll get you out of this . . . this incubator."

Anna felt the woman's fingernails glide over her skin. She sensed that the woman would like to simply tear her stomach open and pluck the fetus out. She imagined that was just what might occur. It would make the child seem less like Anna's baby and more like her own if Anna didn't actually deliver the infant. It would truly be like taking a baby out of an incubator. Anna saw herself bleeding to death, left to die, discarded, thrown in some hole and deserted and forgotten.

The images quickened her already racing heart. She was sure she had broken out in a sweat. The crazed woman would soon realize it and know she was awake. She swallowed back a cry, squeezing down her terror. The woman opened her hand again and lay her palm on Anna's stomach. She rubbed in circles and chanted, "Grow my precious, grow," as if she had some magical power to make the baby develop faster. Then she brought her lips there again.

"Good night, my precious darling," she whispered. "Sleep well and feed."

"What is it, Mommy?" Anna heard the man ask from the doorway. The woman lifted her hand from her stomach as if she had accidentally placed it on a hot stove.

"Nothing. I'm just . . . making sure everything is all right."

"When you didn't come up, I thought something might have happened," he said. "We don't need any more trouble tonight," he added with the tone of a warning. What other trouble did they have? Anna wondered.

"There's no trouble. She ate everything."

"Good. Let's get some sleep now, Mommy. I have a full day at the hospital tomorrow. Tommy's off. I want to be able to get all my work done and get home to my family," he said with a smile in his voice.

"Okay, Daddy."

She pulled Anna's nightgown down and stepped away from the bed to get the tray.

"I'll take that for you," the man said.

"Thank you, Daddy."

Anna sensed they were both still standing there, gazing at her.

"I wish it wasn't going to take so long," the woman said.

"It's not really that long. Look at how long we've waited," he reminded her. She sighed.

"I don't know if it's so good for you to come down here so often, Mommy. It only serves to remind you of the waiting. Maybe I should bring her breakfast tomorrow and every day, and when I'm off, I'll bring her lunch and dinner too."

"No. I want to be sure everything's going all right. I want to see for myself, Daddy. Not that I don't trust you. I just need to be sure. Besides, you have enough to do. You're the sole breadwinner since I stopped working."

"Whatever you want, Mommy. Ready?"

"Yes."

She heard them go to the door, pause, and then leave. The lock clicked; their footsteps died away, and only that grinding was heard. Anna let out a long-held breath, sat up, and thought about her attempt to escape. She knew she would have only one chance, because if she failed, they would strap her down in this bed and keep her like an invalid until the baby could be taken.

She tried to remember the little she had seen about the place when they had first brought her. She knew she had to get to the basement door. If it was locked, she would have to go upstairs to get out. But getting out might not be enough. Where were they? How far from other people? How would she get this horrible thing off her head?

The questions and difficulties seemed to heap

impossibility over her hope, but she had to make the effort. She went to the hook in the wall and loosened it completely so that all that had to be done was tug once to get the chain free. Then she thought about what would happen in the morning.

The woman would come in with her breakfast tray. The woman was stronger than she was, and crazed with a viciousness that would make her a formidable opponent. Anna had to utilize surprise. She could attack her as soon as she came through the door, but if she wasn't in the bed, the woman might become suspicious and cautious.

And what if the man hadn't yet gone? What if she screamed and he came to her aid? Anna certainly couldn't overpower both of them. Moving about with this thing on her head was hard enough as it was. The disadvantages were enormous. She grew more and more depressed thinking about them.

But she sucked in her stomach and clenched her jaw.

I must get out of here tomorrow, she warned herself. *I must try while I still have some strength in my body. A week from now, I'll be even more helpless.*

Going back to sleep was dangerous, she thought. What if she didn't wake up before the woman arrived? She had to keep herself awake, ready, and stir the adrenaline. No sleep, not even dozing.

She started to walk around the room, holding

the chain so it didn't drag on the floor. Periodically she went into the bathroom and ran some cold water. Then she stopped doing that because she was afraid they could hear the water in the pipes.

How much time had passed? Hours? Only minutes? She tried counting, but that started to make her sleepy. She tried singing to herself. She recited psalms she knew by heart. She took the Bible the woman had brought and read from it aloud. She paraded some more, and after she had done all this, she had the terrible, sinking feeling only an hour or so had passed.

I'll be exhausted, she thought. *I'll be too tired to lift a finger in my own defense.*

I've got to get a little sleep, just a little.

She returned to the bed and sprawled on her side, facing the door.

Just a little sleep. Surely, I'll hear the key in the lock again and I'll be ready.

God, give me strength.

Her eyelids grew heavier. She couldn't keep them open.

That grinding, that damnable grinding . . .

She fell asleep dreaming about a giant rodent gnawing its way through the wall to get to her so it could rip out the fetus and consume it.

Thank God for the nightmare, she thought after it woke her. *I might have slept too long.*

She waited, eyes open, staring at the door.

23

When McShane stepped out of Lidia Ambrook's apartment, he saw Frank Reynolds and another FBI agent drive up. They got out of their vehicle and headed toward him, neither looking as if he were in much of a hurry. The other man looked more like an FBI agent, McShane thought. He was tall and broad, with a chiseled face and granite chin. He had a military posture, firm, confident.

"What's the story here?" Reynolds asked without making any introductions.

"The woman I described to you yesterday, Anna Gold's friend, was murdered earlier tonight. Medical examiner thinks the killer injected her with something that brought on heart failure, suffocation. I'm waiting for the autopsy, but he found a trauma on her neck that looks like it was caused by a hypodermic needle, and there is evidence of a struggle."

"Yeah?" Reynolds said as if McShane had just described nothing more important than what he had had for dinner.

"Well, Anna Gold disappears, her friend is murdered—"

"Did you find anything to tie the two events together?"

"Nothing concrete, but I have this feeling—"

"This woman wasn't pregnant too, was she?" the other agent asked.

"Not that I know. Why would they kill a pregnant woman, anyway? That would kill the baby, and they're supposedly in the business of saving babies," McShane said with a smirk.

"They found one of the missing women in Texas. Apparently she had suffered a miscarriage. Her body was left at the door of a church."

"How was she killed?"

"Not with a hypodermic needle. She hemorrhaged and was allowed to bleed to death."

"Two of the fanatics seen in Texas were here during the demonstration at the clinic," Reynolds said.

"But Anna Gold was abducted about the same time the demonstration was taking place."

"I didn't say they were at the demonstration. I said they were here at the time," Reynolds corrected. "A man and a woman, both in their early thirties. They drive a late-model white Ford van, and a van of similar description was seen by a stock clerk at Van's about the time Anna Gold was abducted."

"What clerk? I asked if anyone had seen anything," McShane said.

They both stared at him.

"Sometimes," Reynolds said, "we can get answers local law enforcement doesn't get because we know what questions to ask."

"And people tend to think harder for us," the other agent said.

"Unless you have anything else, this looks like a separate problem," Reynolds added, nodding toward the complex.

"Okay," McShane said, annoyed with their arrogance. "You going to tell Cutler or should I?"

"We'll tell him, but if you come up with anything you think would be of interest . . ."

"You'll be the first to know," McShane said. "So, how is your investigation of Anna Gold's disappearance going, then?"

"We think these people are holed up in a farmhouse outside of Parksville," Reynolds said. "She might very well be in there too."

"Parksville? Anna Gold's family lives there."

"Just a coincidence, I'm sure," Reynolds said. "Anyway, we're keeping the place under surveillance and waiting for the right moment."

"Right moment? What right moment?"

"The one that doesn't turn it into another Waco," the other agent said. "You know how that went and what followed as a result."

McShane nodded. Maybe all this was out of his league.

"Okay. I'll carry on with the assumption this is a separate felony."

"Probably a love affair gone sour," Reynolds said, looking at Lidia Ambrook's apartment.

"Passions run amok," the other agent agreed with a cold smile. "Nine times out of ten."

"Romance has become a dangerous thing nowadays," Reynolds said.

McShane couldn't resist, but he said it with a smile.

"Is that why you have so little of it in your life?"

The other agent laughed. Reynolds shrugged.

"Maybe," he admitted. "See you later, alligator."

McShane watched them return to their vehicle. He thought about what they had told him and what he had theorized. If they were right and they knew who the abductors were and where they were keeping Anna Gold, he was running all over the place, pissing in the wind.

But what if they weren't right?

He looked at his watch. It was a little after eleven. Late, but who could sleep now? He went to his car to use his cellular.

Miriam Gold answered before the second ring.

"Sorry if I woke you," he said quickly. "This is Detective McShane."

"You didn't wake me. I stay up late so I can fall

asleep," she confessed. He liked that honesty and the simplicity of the confession.

"I'm afraid what I'm going to tell you isn't going to help cure your insomnia."

"Something terrible has happened to Anna?"

"No, a friend of hers. I was wondering if she had ever mentioned her: Lidia Ambrook."

"She did mention her, yes. Anna likes her. I had the feeling she was her best friend, or only friend. What happened to her?"

"It looks like she was murdered earlier tonight."

"Oh, no. You think the same people who abducted my sister did that?"

"I don't know yet."

"I thought you were off her case, that it was the FBI who was investigating now."

"It is, but I had interviewed Lidia Ambrook and I had the feeling she might have known Anna's lover."

"Lover?" Miriam said disdainfully. "Yes, I suppose that's what he is, her lover."

"Do you remember anything else Anna might have said about Lidia—anything at all?"

"I don't know. I'd have to sit and think awhile and try to recall our conversations on the phone."

"Okay."

"I guess you haven't been able to get much sleep either," she said, "with all you have to do."

"No," he said, smiling.

"Well, I have this herbal tea my friend Sophia Mendelson gave me. She says it guarantees you a good night's rest."

He laughed.

"You're welcome to try some."

He started to laugh again and then thought, *Why not?*

"It's late," he said, but not convincingly.

"How long will it take you to get here?"

"Actually, I'm only about twenty minutes away. We law enforcement people can push the envelope on the highway."

"Pardon?"

"Go faster than the speed limit."

"Oh. Well, I'll put up the water."

"Isn't your father . . . ?"

"He's asleep. He's always been able to go to sleep when he wants," she said, not disguising her disapproval.

"Be there in eighteen minutes," he told her, and started his engine.

Fifteen minutes later he turned down her road. He pulled into the Golds' driveway less than two minutes later. She was waiting at the door.

"I guess you *do* drive fast," she said, smiling. She wore a light cotton white shawl over her shoulders and had her hair down. It gleamed in the porch light, as did her eyes. "Come in, please," she said, holding the door open.

He stepped into the house and followed her to

the dining room, where she had set out the teacups, a plate of small cakes, lemon, and cream.

"Sit. I'll just get the tea," she said. She moved gracefully to the kitchen. He sat and gazed around the room. When he was here before, he hadn't noticed the oil painting of a rabbi teaching a young boy lessons from the Torah. There was a look of great satisfaction on the elderly rabbi's face and the boy looked studious.

"Nice picture," he said, nodding toward it when she returned with the teakettle.

"My aunt Ethel did that," she said. "My father's youngest sister. She still lives in their old brownstone in Brooklyn."

"Talented lady."

"Yes. There are galleries that have her paintings. She's very fond of Anna and is heartbroken over what has happened between her and my father, but she doesn't know about her being abducted."

He watched her pour the tea into his cup. She had long but very feminine fingers and thin wrists. She smiled at him and poured herself a cup before sitting next to him.

"So, how was this young woman murdered?"

"We think she was injected with something fatal," he replied, and sipped the tea. He nodded: "Good."

"You can put lemon in it or cream, but I think it would be better with lemon," she said.

"Right. Lidia Ambrook appears to be your sister's only friend. She must have been very lonely after she left your home."

"She told me she was lonely here."

"You're not? I don't mean to pry, but . . ."

"No, it's all right to ask. Anna and I are different. Anna was always more rebellious, always demanding answers, never accepting faith on its own. Logic, reason, she insisted. She challenged from the day she could speak, and she was more conscious of what she called our isolation."

"Your isolation?"

Miriam smiled.

"Anna wanted to be more like Reform Jews, whom my father calls gentiles with Jewish names."

"I can understand him being a little upset about it, but to deny her very existence . . ."

"It's the other way around in his mind, Detective. My father cannot separate himself from who he is, and so he believes Anna has denied his existence."

"Pardon?"

"To deny the tenets of our faith, he thinks, is to deny him. You see, Jews everywhere think of themselves as members of the same family. We are all sons and daughters of Abraham, and like any member of a family, you have to accept its burdens and its tribulations. 'You shall be to Me a kingdom of priests and a holy nation.' It's our destiny, you see, to serve God, spend time studying Torah, faithfully observing the ritual and ethical commandments.

"To my father," Miriam continued, "for Anna to deny her faith was to deny her existence, so when she turned her back on the rituals and denied the commandments, he viewed her as committing suicide. And so, he mourns her death."

"Did you try to talk him out of that?"

She smiled softly and shook her head.

"You don't talk my father out of anything. You make him see that he agrees," she said. McShane laughed. "I tried to get him to see her as in need of his love and not rejecting it. I tried to get him to feel she needs him more, but he's not a patient man, nor is he as forgiving as he wants to be.

"After you told us what happened to her, he went into prayer and has been doing nothing else. I know he's praying for her, although he won't admit it to me."

"You're obviously a great asset to him at this time of his life."

"I do what I have to do," she said. " 'Honor thy father and mother.' "

He nodded and reached for one of the cakes.

"Very good. Homemade?"

She nodded.

"*Rugelah.* You've had it before?"

"If I have, it wasn't this good," he said. She blushed. "So, did you give any more thought to Lidia Ambrook and your sister?"

"I remember Anna telling me that Lidia was really hooked on astrology."

"Right."

"And that she was preparing charts on her and the man she was with."

McShane dipped into his pocket and unfolded the paper that had the chart. He handed it to Miriam. She nodded.

"I found that, along with some others, in Lidia Ambrook's apartment. It might very well be Anna's lover's chart, then."

"Yes, I think so too."

"At least we know his date of birth," McShane said, taking back the paper.

"Not very much, is it?"

"No, but it's something."

He drank more tea and finished his cake.

"What does your wife think about your working so long and so late? I imagine it's difficult for her."

"Very," he said. "We're at the beginning of a divorce."

"Oh, I'm sorry."

"Me too. I think," he said.

"You're not sure?"

"My wife told me I don't believe in anything enough. I suppose that goes for my marriage too."

"You're not religious?"

"Hardly. Can't remember the last time I went to church. Oh, yeah, I do: to get married," he said. He smiled but she didn't.

"If you don't believe in anything, you can't believe in yourself," Miriam said. He thought for a moment and nodded.

"Funny," he said, gazing around. "Here we are, dealing with people who are fanatical about their beliefs to the point where they're willing to die or kill others to sustain them, and here I am, investigating these people, and I'm accused of believing in nothing."

"Maybe that's the sort of a person it takes," Miriam said, smiling. "It's all very simple for you.

"But afterward, Detective, when you have your quiet moment, you will have to turn to something. If you have no marriage, if you have no faith, what will you turn to?"

"I don't know," he said.

"How do you feel about that?"

He thought a moment.

"A little scared," he admitted.

"Good," she said. He tilted his head, confused. "It's because of fear that we have so great a need for faith. I'm sure," she added, her eyes down, "my poor sister is having similar thoughts right now, wherever she is being held prisoner."

He nodded.

"Come back after you have rescued her," Miriam said, "and argue with my father. He'll get you to believe in something."

McShane laughed. "I might just do that."

"Good," she said. She fixed those penetrating eyes on him and he felt warm and comfortable. "A little tired?"

"Huh?"

"The tea?"

"Oh. Yeah. Thanks," he said. "I'd better get going. I have a lot to do tomorrow."

"I imagine so," she said. She followed him to the door.

"Thanks again for the tea. And the *rug* . . ."

"*Rugelah*," she said, laughing.

"Right. Good night."

He stepped out and down the stairs. He turned at the car and looked back at her.

After you rescue my sister, she had said.

He'd like to be able to do that, he thought, if it wasn't already too late.

24

Anna's eyes were still open when she heard the sound of footsteps outside the door. Her heart pounded in anticipation of what she was about to attempt. She had the chain down on the left side of her body, her hand under the blanket, clutching the heavy links. All she had to do was give the chain a good tug and it would come flying out of the wall, enabling her to move freely and get out of the room.

For the remainder of the night, she had gone over and over the escape, replayed the scene in her mind, studying it carefully. She choreographed her every movement and considered options, complications. She realized she would never again have the confidence she had now. She had to succeed; it had to work just as she had designed it in her imagination.

When Anna heard the key being inserted into

the lock, her fingers tightened on the chain. The door swung open and the woman appeared, breakfast tray in hand. She was dressed in a robe and slippers and looked half asleep herself. That was good, Anna thought: She was not alert.

As the woman entered the room Anna turned her head slightly. Ironically the iron box over her head now served as an aid: It hid her eyes from the woman, so the woman couldn't see that Anna was fully awake. She gazed quickly at Anna and moved toward the table to put down the tray. The moment she turned away from the bed, Anna jerked the chain. It flew up from the wall, sounding like a bullet when it snapped in the air.

Surprised, shocked, the woman froze with her mouth open and stared at the chain as though it were alive. Anna swung her feet over the bed and charged forward, her head down, the metal box like a ramrod, and struck the woman as she was turning, hitting her on her left side, just under her ribs.

The tray sailed over the woman's head to crash on the table, dishes, cup, and glass cascading over the edge, and the woman, taken completely by surprise, followed, falling backward, hitting the table, and toppling over the right side of it to the floor. The table turned over and fell on her.

She howled.

Anna yanked in the chain frantically until it was bunched in her hands and ran toward the door.

Recovering her wits, the woman crawled to her feet and lunged, grabbing Anna at her shoulders just as she made it to the doorway.

Anna was screaming too now. She had become a clawing, desperate animal battling for survival. She tried to push the woman off with her right hand, but the woman then took hold of the metal box and used her leverage to drag Anna back from the door.

"No! You can't leave; you can't take my baby away!"

Anna swung her left hand, which clutched the chain. Most of it was gathered in something of a ball, the remainder of it dangling like a whip. She struck the woman with it on the side of the head and it stunned her and sliced her skin, driving her back. The blood flowed down the side of her face.

"My baby!" she moaned, tears in her eyes. She felt the side of her head and saw the blood on her fingers. It froze her for the moment. "Daddy!" she cried.

Terrified that the man would soon appear, Anna didn't hesitate. She turned and rushed out the door, still clutching the chain in her left hand.

The fieldstone basement had only a naked light-bulb dangling at the bottom of the wooden stairway, but there was enough illumination to show her the avenues of escape. Anna moved quickly to the door she recalled led to the cement steps; however, it was as she had feared: locked.

When the woman appeared in the bedroom doorway behind her, Anna rushed to the stairs and climbed as quickly as she could, her bare feet pounding down on the old wooden steps. She'd get past the man too, if he was there, she told herself. The woman swung around the base of the stairway to charge up after her. Anna got to the door and opened it, stepping into a narrow hallway.

She wasn't sure whether she should go right or left, but she knew it was only a matter of seconds before the woman would be at her again. Thank God, the man apparently wasn't there, she thought. Instinctively, Anna turned back to the basement door and opened it just as the woman reached the top of the stairway. She struck the woman again, this time directly at the center of her forehead. Her reappearing like that took the woman by surprise, and she didn't block the blow. It sent her reeling backward, tripping and falling down the steps, giving Anna the time she desperately needed.

Totally disoriented, Anna rushed to her right, which brought her to the kitchen instead of the front of the house. Fortunately there was a door at the rear. She went out and down a small stairway and turned to her right. The house was apparently surrounded by woods on all sides but one, where there was a rather wide stream. When she came around the corner of the building, she realized what that grinding sound had been. She ran past it toward the front of the house, where she could see a hard, dirt road.

The woman was screaming behind her, still inside.

"My baby! She's taking my baby! Stop her!"

Oblivious to the small stones and gravel cutting the bottom of her feet, Anna decided to run to her left down the road, hoping to find a neighboring house quickly and get help, but the road seemed to lead deeper and deeper into the woods, with no signs of human habitation.

She heard the woman produce an ugly, guttural cry and turned to see her pursuing.

"Help me," Anna whimpered, and continued to sprint ahead, her feet screaming, the metal box on her head quickly becoming heavier and heavier with every step taken. The dirt road eventually came to an end, after which there was just forest.

"Oh, no," she muttered. She had trapped herself. She saw the woman coming, her hands fisted, her robe open, exposing her nudity. She had somehow lost her slippers in pursuit and she, too, was running barefoot, but she also seemed oblivious to pain.

Rather than face her to do battle again, Anna lunged into the forest. High bushes caught on the nightgown, some branches with thorns cutting through to rip at her thighs, but she didn't stop. She plowed through them into a clearing and ran harder. Her left foot sank into a hole and she fell forward, slamming hard against the ground. It was as if a knife had been brought to her ankle. For a moment she lost her breath and her equilibrium, but she could hear the crazed woman behind her, tearing through the bushes, screaming, "My baby! My baby!"

Anna pushed herself to her feet and went left between two birch trees, limping to avoid the pain in her ankle. The forest was thicker here and the earth cooler to her feet and not as rocky, but the pain in her right side that emanated from her frantic lungs soaked through her ribs and down to her abdomen. Her lungs felt as if they would burst. Her throat was closing. When she looked down at her feet, she saw they were all bloodied.

After rounding a large old oak, she paused to listen. The woman wasn't screaming after her anymore. Maybe she had given up, Anna thought. Maybe she was confused and had gone off in the wrong direction. The forest was so quiet; it was as if all life had left it. She peered through the trees on her left and then on her right. There was no sign of her pursuer. It gave her a chance to take some deep breaths. The pain in her ankle subsided. At least it wasn't broken, she thought.

Slightly revived, she moved slowly, cautiously, as quietly as she could to her left. The ground started to slope upward, but she hoped she could get to a point where she could see her surroundings and know better in which direction she should go. This part of the forest was full of pine. It smelled fresh, clean, and the earth was carpeted with the fallen needles and cones. A squirrel appeared to her right, studied her for a moment, and then scurried to its left and ran up a tree quickly to peer down at her, its nose twitching.

She smiled.

"I'm going to make it," she muttered. "I'm going to be all right."

The forest seemed to end abruptly after ten more yards. She was on a rockier slope and could see a precipice just ahead. She hurried up to it to get a good view of the area. There had to be a road nearby, a house—something.

The ground was soft at the edge. Some of it crumbled under her weight and cascaded to the rocks below. She backed up but remained there, studying the woods, and sure enough, she saw a cottage about a half a mile or so to her right.

"Thank God," she said, and turned to head that way just as the crazed woman, crouching like a Neanderthal, her arms dangling, her hands like claws, came running out of the pine forest. Her voice was caught in a shrill scream of madness and anger.

She, too, had been slashed and scratched by the undergrowth. Her legs were striped with blood, the right sleeve of her robe torn. The blood that had come when Anna had slapped the chain against her temple was caked over her cheek, and the trickle that came from the blow Anna had delivered on the stairway ran down the bridge of the woman's nose. She resembled some primitive warrior woman painted for battle.

Anna backed up, not sure whether she should go to her right or her left. Every move she made, the woman anticipated and countered, like a collegiate wrestler. She drew closer, her eyes wide.

"You can't take my baby," she said in a raspy voice. She smiled. "You're not going to take my baby."

Anna lunged to her right and the woman leaped forward. This time she was ready for Anna's blow and blocked Anna's left hand so that the bundled chain wouldn't strike her. At the same time she seized the collar with her left hand and swung Anna around sharply. Anna fell to the ground and the woman kicked her hard in the back. Anna collapsed forward. The woman straddled her. She took hold of the metal box and jerked it up, the metal now cutting into Anna's throat. Gagging, she reached for the woman's hands and tried to pull them away, but the woman seemed stronger than ever.

"Get up slowly and start back," she ordered. She tugged to get Anna to her knees. Anna started to rise. All she could think was that she couldn't go back, she mustn't go back. She spun as she rose, screaming madly herself, her right hand balled into a fist, and caught the woman in the throat with her blow. It drove her to the left and she fell. Anna rushed to take advantage of the opportunity and started away, but the woman reached desperately and caught hold of the chain, hauling it back with such force that the collar around Anna's neck snapped her head and throat, knocking the breath out of her. She was gasping when the woman curled the chain around her hand and held it like a leash.

It's over, Anna thought, fighting for air. *I can't do it.*

"Get to your feet and walk. Do it!"

Anna shook her head.

"I'll drag you back, then," she said, and started away. The chain tightened and the collar dug into her throat again. Without choice, Anna crawled on her hands and knees.

"You're like a dog," the woman sneered.

Still on her hands and knees, Anna contemplated her for a moment, her rage building from the base of her stomach into her chest. With her last vestige of self-respect and dignity coming to the fore, her last-ditch hope to live emerging, she gathered one more surge of strength and, still on her hands and knees, charged again at the woman like a defensive tackle, this time striking her with the metal box just under her knees. She fell backward, and the edge of the precipice, which was only a soft block of earth, gave way. The woman sank quickly through it and began to fall.

She screamed. The earth continued to crumble faster with her clumsy effort to prevent herself from going over, and then after a moment she was gone.

But she hadn't let go of the chain. It snapped in the air and pulled the collar, driving Anna down and toward the same fatal edge. She grabbed it with both her hands and tried to alleviate the pressure by pulling back on it. She was suddenly in the ironic position of either saving the woman by getting her back up, choking to death, or following her over the edge.

She didn't have the strength to haul the woman back up. The woman's weight dragged Anna forward until she was looking over the precipice. The woman dangled below. It was only about a hundred and fifty feet to the bottom, but the bottom was all jagged rock. Anna struggled to find something to stop her from sliding. There was just a small tree, barely a sapling. She seized it, and for a moment it held.

Anna could see that the woman's hands were all bloodied, yet she still managed to clutch the chain. The sapling was being torn out of the earth.

"Let go!" Anna screamed down at her. "Or you'll kill the baby!"

The madness evaporated from the woman's face. She gazed up thoughtfully for a moment, and then released her grip on the chain.

She fell without a scream and bounced hard on

the rocks below, bouncing from one edge to another, her body snapping and twisting until it came to a stop over some large rocks. She didn't move, didn't twitch.

Anna closed her eyes and then rose to her knees, drawing the chain back. When she had it bundled in her hand, she stood up, wobbled a bit, and then headed down toward the small house she had seen.

But the fatigue and the effort rushed over her with a vengeance. Every step took a greater and greater effort. She stumbled often and tripped once, slamming down hard on some small rocks. They sliced her left arm badly. The pain was excruciating. It took the breath out of her again. She lay there, thinking maybe she would just sleep a few moments, rest, and gather some strength, but something moved in the bushes behind her and she had the horrid vision of that woman, battered and bleeding, still coming after her.

She struggled to her feet once again, and once again she plodded along, moving down the wooded slope. Before she reached the clearing she had seen from the distance, a long, sharp pain cut across her abdomen. It resembled a kick in the stomach. She crouched over, aching, moaning.

"Help," she muttered. "Someone, help me, please."

Only able to take short, slow steps now, it seemed to take ages for her to emerge from the woods. She felt the warm trickle of blood down the inside of her thighs.

"Oh, God, no," she said. She put all her remaining strength into a few more steps, which brought her to the clearing, and then she fell forward, passing out before she hit the grass, never hearing the yapping golden retriever that had raised its head and leaped off the swinging seat on the porch of the small cottage.

25

McShane decided that immediately after breakfast he would take another ride to the house belonging to the couple Royce claimed wanted Anna Gold's unborn baby. Perhaps he would be able to tell more, see more in daylight. He had just sat in a booth at the diner and opened the menu when his beeper went off. He had to call in to the station.

"Where are you?" Mark Ganner asked.

"Diner. Why?"

"You got to get to Mountaindale, the Sandburg Creek road, a place belonging to a John Allan. Paramedics are on their way."

"To what?"

"This is bizarre. This John Allan claims his dog found a woman in the field near the house a little while ago."

"Dead?"

"Not dead, but in bad shape, lots of blood, but that's not the weird part."

"What?"

"She has a collar around her neck with a chain and, according to Allan, a metal box locked over her head with holes for eyes, ears, nose, and mouth."

"I'm on my way," McShane said, and hurried out to his car. He swung onto the Quickway and slapped on his bubble light. He took the Rock Hill exit, hitting ninety-five along the way, and drove toward Glen Wild and a side road he knew led into Mountaindale. The way he drove, it was fortunate the tourist season had ended and it was early in the morning. He took turns on the wrong side of the road and drove about twenty miles past the sensible speed for a twisted back highway peppered with potholes. A few times he almost lost control and went into a ditch.

Mountaindale was nearly a ghost town, especially after the summer. One of the smaller resort hamlets, it had lost nearly all of its bungalow colonies and small hotels to the economic downturn. Most of the stores were boarded shut. There was so little traffic that the light was no longer working at the center of the hamlet. The streets were deserted, but luckily one of the hamlet's oldtimers, an elderly, bald man with two patches of gray at his temples, was making his way toward the old synagogue briskly, despite the fact that he was walking with a cane. McShane honked his horn and pulled up beside him.

"Excuse me," he said.

"Yes?"

"You know a John Allan?"

"Of course I know John Allan. John Allan was town assessor longer than you're old. Is there a fire at his house? I just saw the ambulance follow the fire truck going in that direction."

"No, not a fire. Where's his house exactly?"

The old man lifted the cane and pointed.

"Follow the Spring Glen road a mile and a half and turn left on Sandburg Creek. He's the third house on the right. Tell him Dave Malisoff sent you. I used to be the mayor."

"Thanks. I'll tell him," McShane said, and shot off. He nearly drove past the Sandburg Creek road. He had to hit the brakes hard and the car spun around on some gravel. He accelerated and climbed the hill, which then descended rapidly toward the creek. The road ran along the creek for another couple of miles before the first house appeared. There were people standing in the front, looking in the direction of the Allan residence. The same was true for the second house. All had been roused by the sirens and commotion, which fell like heavy thunder on the otherwise peaceful rural setting.

McShane saw the ambulance in the driveway ahead and the fire truck right beside it. He pulled up quickly and hurried out. One of the volunteer firemen was standing by the fire truck with the radio phone in his hand.

"What's happening?" McShane said, looking toward the half-dozen men gathered in the field.

"Trying to get a locksmith to meet us at the hospital. Jesus, what a sight," he said.

McShane ran toward the group. They lifted Anna Gold onto the stretcher and began to make their way back toward the ambulance.

"How is she?"

"Pretty bad," one of the paramedics said. "It looks like she was pregnant and she aborted."

"It must be Anna Gold," McShane said. He moved to the stretcher and walked along, revolted by the weird sight himself. "Can she talk?" he asked the paramedic. "Did she tell you her name?"

"She's incoherent, in shock."

"Did she say anything at all?"

"Something about a wheel in the water . . . Mommy falling off a cliff." He shook his head. "She's been through hell. All sorts of contusions and traumas. Her feet are slashed. She looks like she ran miles. She came out of the woods back there. Ask the old man about it: He found her," he said, nodding toward a tall man with a tanned face and a shock of thick gray hair.

McShane nodded.

"She going to make it?"

"Blood pressure's low. I'm not sure what other internal injuries there are," the paramedic said.

McShane stopped walking beside them and they continued to the ambulance. He watched them for a moment. John Allan joined him.

"Damn craziest thing I ever did see," he said.

"Mr. Allan, I'm Detective McShane," he said showing his ID quickly. "What happened?"

"Well, I don't know exactly. I heard my dog yapping like mad and came out. She was standing over something in the field and barking. I couldn't make anything out from the porch, so I walked down and saw her just lying there, moaning. I ran back to the house as fast as I could and called for an ambulance and the police. I told 'em to bring up a torch or something to get that box off her head and collar off her neck. There's a chain too. You see it?"

"Yeah. You didn't see anyone else?"

"No, sir, but I didn't look around. Coulda been someone in the woods back there. I don't know. Damn crazy thing," he said, shaking his head. His eyes were still glassy from the shock and excitement.

"Paramedics said she mumbled something about a wheel in the water. That make any sense to you?"

"Wheel in the water?" He thought a moment and then nodded, his face brightening. "Sure does."

"What does it mean?"

"Gristmill, down at the end of the road. It's the last place on the right, the old Corning place. . . . Makes sense," he said, nodding again. "That's why she come out of the woods from that direction."

"Anyone live there?"

"Yeah, a married couple. One of the Corning girls, Judith. She was in the Army, a nurse, for a while. Her husband's in medicine too. He's a lab technician over at the hospital. Name's Gary, Gary Dunbar."

"Do they have any children?"

"No, sir, they don't. They're loners, keep to themselves, don't so much as wave when they drive past. Margaret and Jack Corning were kinda like that too. My wife, Ruth, she died two years ago, was the only one on the street talked much to Margaret, but she never liked her."

"Thanks," McShane said. He returned to his car and radioed the station. "Tell the sheriff I believe we've located Anna Gold. They're taking her to the hospital. It looks like she might have been held by a couple named Gary and Judith Dunbar. They live just past the Allan residence. I'm heading over there now."

"You wanna wait for backup? Billy's on his way."

"I'll be fine," he said. "But tell him to keep coming."

He pulled out and continued down the back road, which lost any trace of macadam after a while and was just hard-packed dirt and gravel. The two-story house soon came into view and he saw the gristmill right behind it. The front door of the house appeared to be wide open. He drove up slowly, stared a moment to see if anyone would appear, and then turned off the engine. He sat there, waiting. It was deadly quiet.

Cautiously, he stepped out of the vehicle and reached back to unfasten his pistol. He started toward the front door, watching both sides of the house as he walked. On the porch he listened again. There was just the heavy, monotonous sound of the gristmill turning in the water.

"Hello?" he said, knocking on the doorjamb. He waited, listened, and then pounded again with his closed fist. Nothing. Anxious now, he took out his pistol and entered the house. Despite the bright day, the house was dank and dark, all the window shades drawn down, no lights on. The living room on his right was full of shadows created by the illumination that leaked in and around the drawn curtains. He gazed into the dining room and went on to the kitchen. The back door was open, so he went to it and peered out.

A loud creak in the building spun him around. His heart was pounding, and for a moment his eyes played tricks on him. He thought someone was standing in the kitchen doorway, but it was only an apron hooked on the door. He listened and then stepped out back. The yard was overgrown, and he could see where someone had trampled the high grass. He followed the path, which led him around and back to the front of the house.

He paused, listened, and gazed up at the curtained windows. One window was open and a piece of the curtain flapped in and out.

"Anyone here?"

The sound of the stream, the gristmill, and some crows cawing was all he heard. He returned to the house and went down the hall toward the stairway, pausing when he saw the open door to the basement. Cautiously he looked down the basement steps. There was a light on, the bulb fixture and bulb dangling from the ceiling. The basement itself didn't look like much from where he stood. It had a hard dirt floor with nothing covering the stone foundation.

Nevertheless, the fact that the light was still on indicated that someone had been there recently. He started down the stairs. The old wooden steps groaned under his weight. He paused at the bottom and looked around, surprised to see another door and what looked like another room, but a room built independently of the basement, obviously tacked on at a much later time.

"Anyone down here?" he called. The silence filled him with trepidation. Maybe he should have waited for Billy before exploring this house. Another loud creak in the building spun him around toward the stairway, but there was no one there. Slowly he approached the doorway of this add-on room and gazed through it.

A bedroom with a bathroom—how curious, he thought—and then he saw the table turned over, the dishes shattered, the food splattered over the floor. He entered the room and noticed the hook over the bed and the fact that there were no windows.

It looked like a prison cell, he thought, gazing at the stark white walls. This was surely where they had kept her.

He hurried out of the room and up the basement stairs. Then he climbed the stairway to the second story and bedrooms. He peered into what was obviously a baby's nursery and looked at all the furniture, the stuffed animals, the paraphernalia for infants. Some of it looked brand-new; some of it look faded, old.

He continued to the second bedroom, which was obviously the master bedroom. The bed was unmade, a closet wide open. He stood there for a moment, listening. Then he entered the room, checked the bathroom, and started to look at things on the dresser and vanity table. He opened the drawer to one of the night tables and perused the contents. He was about to close it when something caught his eye: a telephone number on an index card and a business card attached. He studied it for a moment and then put it in his pocket. So much for the FBI's theory that this was part of a national conspiracy, he thought.

The sound of a car driving up spun him around and sent him out and down the stairs. Billy Slater got out of a patrol car just as McShane stepped out of the house.

"What d'ya got?"

"The woman found in the field was Anna Gold. I'm sure these people were the ones who had abducted her. She was kept here, shut up in the basement, but she escaped, running through the woods toward the Allan place," he said, pointing with his pistol. "I've checked it out. There's no one here now, but from what the paramedics said, she mumbled something about someone going over a cliff. My guess is she was pursued through the woods, either by one or both of them. Better get some reinforcements for a search party. Keep your eyes peeled in case one of them appears. These are very strange and dangerous people."

"Right." Billy reached for his radio phone and McShane reentered the house and went to the kitchen, where he had seen a telephone on the wall.

When it rang three or four times, he thought no one was home, but then Miriam Gold picked up.

"Your sister's been found," he said. "She apparently escaped by herself, but she's injured. They've taken her to the hospital emergency room."

"Oh, my God. I'll go there immediately."

"It's not a pretty story," he warned. "Brace yourself."

"I've been prepared ever since you came to our door," she replied.

He smiled.

"I imagine you have," he said. "I'll see you there."

"Thank you."

"Where you going?" Billy asked when he came charging out of the house and toward his car.

"To finish solving the case," he replied. "There's one loose end I want to stitch up myself." The anger building inside him painted his face crimson.

He shot away, spitting gravel, his bubble light going.

It wasn't until he was through Mountaindale that his rage cooled enough for him to realize that he had better make one more stop first. What if only the woman had been chasing Anna Gold through the woods?

He had better go to the hospital, he thought.

26

Gary Dunbar pushed his cart out of the elevator on the third floor, heading for rooms 303, 307, and 308 to get blood samples for lab work. He wasn't thinking about anything in particular. In fact, he was a bit drowsy this morning. He had fallen asleep quickly the night before, especially after all the wine they had drunk and the loving way she had massaged him with her skin oil. However, Mommy was very restless and twice had gotten up during the night. The last time was close to daylight. He knew she was experiencing another one of her anxiety attacks. It always got worse when they had a new incubator downstairs for a few days.

"Something always goes wrong," she told him. "We get so close and then something always goes wrong."

"It won't happen this time," he reassured her. "We're doing it all right."

She agreed, but she couldn't shake off the anxiety. He knew that as time went by and they got closer and closer to the delivery, she would get even worse. He was preparing himself for that; he had stockpiled the tranquilizers. He decided he would start his vacation at the beginning of the ninth month and be home all the time. Once it was all a success and they had their baby, Mommy's anxiety problem would be solved forever. Nothing succeeds like success, he thought, and remained confident.

He had practically sleepwalked through breakfast. Mommy didn't get up to eat with him as she usually did. He had to go upstairs to tell her he was finished and would be leaving for work. When she saw the time, she jumped up and rushed to get the food downstairs.

"Why didn't you wake me?" she demanded.

"I knew you needed your rest, Mommy," he told her, but she was angry at him and wouldn't say good-bye, have a nice day, as she usually did. He expected she would be calmed down by the time he phoned her in the afternoon, but he also expected she would lecture him at dinner and chastise him for not putting the baby's needs before their own.

"A good parent is one who sacrifices constantly for his or her children," she would tell him again and again. He laughed to himself, anticipating. She was sure to illustrate with the bird's nest on the back porch. "Look at how those birds spend every ounce of energy feeding their young. There's nothing else in life for them until their offspring can take care of themselves. Learn from nature, Daddy. It's one of the benefits of living out here."

He'd agree and apologize and promise never to let it happen again, but that wouldn't stop the anxiety attacks. Only the little blue pills would do that, he thought sadly.

He chugged along the corridor toward the nurse's station, where he noticed the entire floor staff, nurse's aides as well as nurses, gathered around the counter, jabbering. Why were they always so full of gossip? Why did they always have so much to say to each other? he wondered, not wholly unenvious.

"Gary," Martha Atwood called to him as he approached, "did you hear about the woman they brought into the emergency room this morning?"

"How would I hear?" he replied. "I was in the lab, getting myself ready."

She smirked, but she was too excited not to talk—as were the others, he noticed curiously.

"She had a metal box locked over her head. Some sort of horrible mask, and a collar with a chain attached on her neck. It's the woman in today's front-page story," she added, holding up the local paper. "The one who had been abducted from the Van's Supermarket lot, Anna Gold."

Gary felt the blood drain from his face.

"She apparently escaped from her captors," one of the nurse's aides added. "She was pregnant, but she aborted and went into shock."

"Didn't you get the call to go down?" Shirley Morris asked.

He shook his head.

"Not yet, or else Margaret Downing was called," he said, but the sound of his voice was foreign, distant. He felt like two people, one cringing inside, the other putting on a face and performance for the nurses and the aides.

"Gruesome, what some people will do to other people," Shirley said, and they all resumed their chatter at once.

Gary gazed ahead at his assignments. He pushed his cart, but when he reached the corner he turned left instead of right and moved quickly toward the exit, which brought him to a service elevator. As soon as the doors opened, he got in and pushed the button for the basement level. There was a phone near the entrance to pathology.

His heart racing, he dialed home and waited as it rang and rang. Finally a man said hello.

"Who is this?" he demanded.

"Bill Slater, sheriff's deputy. Who's this?"

Gary cradled the receiver quickly.

Where was Mommy? How did Anna escape? Their baby was gone, really gone?

He realized there wasn't much time. He had to do something and do it quickly. Less than ten minutes

later, armed with enough potassium chloride to initiate heart failure, he hurried toward the emergency
room.

When he got there, he saw the police in the lobby
and the metal mask, which had been removed, along
with the collar and the chain, being gathered and
studied by a few of them. He approached the nurse
on duty, a tall, slim black woman named Adamson.
She was always friendly but not very warm to him.

"What happened to the woman they found?" he
asked. "I just heard the story upstairs."

"Horrible."

"Is she still alive?"

"Yes, but she's fallen into a coma. We had to get
her into ICU and start a blood transfusion.
Gruesome thing."

He nodded and walked toward the elevator. He
returned to the lab, retrieved his cart, and headed
for the second-floor ICU just about the time
McShane pulled into the emergency-room parking
area.

Leo Hallmark greeted him at the doorway.

"I guess you found your missing woman," he
said. "They sure put her through hell."

"How is she?"

"I don't know."

"Come with me, Leo. We have more to do,"
McShane told the deputy. McShane went directly
to the nurse's station. "How's Anna Gold?" he
asked Barbara Adamson, showing her his ID.

"She wasn't stabilized when they took her to ICU," she explained.

"Do you know a lab technician named Dunbar?"

"Gary? Sure."

McShane leaned over the counter.

"Has he been down here?"

"Just a little while ago. Why?"

"Did he ask about Anna Gold or treat her in any way?"

"He asked about her, yes. But someone else did the blood work."

"Where can I find him? Police emergency," he added.

"I'll call hematology," she said, and picked up the phone. He waited while she inquired. "He's on his rounds," she told McShane. "Third floor."

"Thanks. And Anna Gold's in ICU, which is . . . ?"

"Second floor."

"Thanks. Come on, Leo."

"Who's this Gary Dunbar?"

"One of her captors," McShane told him.

"No shit?"

McShane hurried toward the elevator, wondering if he had gotten to the hospital ahead of Miriam Gold.

He hadn't.

She was in the ICU waiting area with her father, who had surprised her by insisting he go along. The nurse had promised to call them in as soon as they had Anna set up inside, but the minutes seemed like hours to her. She couldn't sit. Harry Gold stared ahead at the door to the ICU, all the anger he had directed toward his daughter now focused on the monsters who had done this terrible thing to her.

He saw Gary Dunbar wheel his cart to the entrance of the ICU and go inside, but of course he thought nothing of it. Moments later McShane and Leo Hallmark appeared. When McShane saw Harry there, he smiled at Miriam, who smiled back.

"How's she doing?"

"They haven't permitted us to go in yet and no one has spoken to us—no doctor."

"These people who did this horrible thing . . . you'll get them?" Harry demanded.

"Absolutely," McShane said. "In fact, I'm here to arrest one of them."

"He works here?" Miriam asked, astounded.

"Lab technician."

"Lab technician?" Harry asked, his eyes widening.

"Yes. He's on the third floor. I just wanted to see you first. Hang in there," he said, clutching Miriam's hands between his and shaking them. He nodded at Harry before he and Leo started back toward the elevator.

"Mr. Detective?" Harry called to him.

"Yes, Mr. Gold."

"I think I saw a lab technician go into the ICU just a minute ago."

McShane froze, looked at Leo, and then ran to the door of the ICU, Leo right behind him. The moment he opened it and they stepped in, a nurse was at them.

"You can't come in here now. Visitors are permitted only five minutes before the hour and—"

"Where's Anna Gold?" McShane demanded. She didn't respond quickly enough, so he charged past her, Leo at his side as he looked at the patients and into the units until he saw Gary Dunbar hovering near Anna Gold across the room on his left.

"That's got to be Dunbar," he said and screamed, *"Dunbar!"*

Gary Dunbar turned, hypodermic needle in hand. The nurse adjusting the intravenous flow looked up as well. Dunbar gazed at Anna Gold a moment and then back at McShane and Leo Hallmark, who walked toward him slowly, Leo moving to the left.

The nurses stood by, shocked and confused by the scene playing out before them.

"Get away from her!" McShane commanded.

Dunbar clutched the hypodermic like a dagger and faced them.

"Easy, Leo," McShane said. The nurse beside Gary gasped and stepped away. "Put that down, Mr. Dunbar. It's over now."

Gary shifted his gaze from Leo to McShane and then turned the hypodermic toward himself. As he jabbed it into his own heart, McShane and Leo

Hallmark rushed him. McShane seized Dunbar's arm before Dunbar could push on the plunger. With Leo's help, they drew his hand away from the hypodermic and McShane pulled it out.

Dunbar struggled, but Leo had him firmly in a bear hug and wrestled him to the floor. The two of them quickly pulled his arms behind his back and put on the handcuffs.

A small circle of blood soaked through the breast of his lab jacket.

McShane looked up at the nurse.

"Treat this, will you," he said. "I need him alive."

"Why did he do that?" the nurse demanded of McShane.

"He was about to do it to her," he said, nodding at Anna Gold. "He's one of the people who kept her captive."

She cringed back.

One of the doctors was at his side a moment later and started to examine Dunbar.

"I guess," McShane said, standing and turning to another nurse who had approached, "if he was going to do something like this to himself, he couldn't have picked a better place for it."

Her eyes widened and she gazed down at Dunbar and the doctor squatting beside him, who started to shout orders.

"Stay with him, Leo," McShane said. Leo nodded.

McShane looked one more time at Anna Gold

and left the ICU. Miriam and Harry Gold were just outside the door.

"It's all right," he told them. "We stopped him. Mr. Gold," he said, "you saved your daughter's life."

Harry's eyes watered. He nodded and reached for Miriam's comforting hand.

"Thank you," she whispered to McShane.

"I've got a little more cleaning up to do," he said. "I'll be back."

Before he left the hospital, he stopped to call the station and fill the sheriff in on what had happened.

"We just got a call a few minutes ago from Billy. John Allan knows the land around there all right: He led them to a cliff and they found Judith Dunbar smashed and broken on some rocks below. Reynolds is checking to see if they're members of the Shepherds of God."

"They're not," McShane said with certainty. "They might be sympathetic to the cause, but they work for themselves," he said, "and someone else."

"Who?"

"Let me surprise you," he told him, and hung up before Ralph Cutler could insist.

Twenty minutes later McShane entered Robert Royce's law office just as the high-profile attorney was preparing to leave for a lunch date.

"This won't take long," McShane told him. He followed him back into his plush office.

"I hope not," Royce said. "I'm having lunch with

some pretty important state politicians. Seems there's a move on to get me to run for Congress," he said, smiling. "I don't know if I could afford the cut in salary, though," he added, sitting down behind his desk.

"Makes sense," McShane said, hovering near the cherry-wood desk.

"Makes sense?" Royce smiled.

"Motive: You can't run for political office if you're exposed as an adulterer who has impregnated an innocent young woman and then had her abducted."

Royce's smile evaporated.

"What the hell are you talking about?"

"Anna Gold. They were going to keep her baby, which would have gotten you off the hook, and afterward we know what they would have done about her, don't we? Then there is the little matter of Lidia Ambrook's murder, which I'm sure you got Gary Dunbar to commit. You knew she could tie Anna to you."

Royce stared.

"Now hold on here—"

"That map you drew, the people you sent me to observe . . . people you claimed wanted to adopt her baby . . . you did that just to put me on the wrong trail. Clever, but no gold ring."

"You don't expect me to believe you can actually prove any of this, do you?"

"I guess you haven't heard the news yet. Anna

Gold escaped from the home of Gary and Judith Dunbar."

Royce remained poker-faced.

"I see. And she told you I was her lover?"

"No, she's still in a coma. I found this at the Dunbar house," McShane said, and tossed the index card with Royce's cellular number and business card attached over the desk. Royce gazed at it.

"What's this prove?"

"That you put them on her. I'm sure I'm not going to have difficulty tying you to them."

"Doesn't mean anything."

"Doesn't it? What about when Dunbar talks, explains how he knew Anna Gold was pregnant and how you helped them with the details of the abduction? Think the district attorney will feel he has a case? You and he don't exactly have a love affair under way either, do you?"

Royce turned a bit pale.

"These people are crazy. You can't believe what they say."

"It doesn't matter what I believe. It's what the jury will believe. Get up," McShane ordered.

"Now, wait a minute . . ."

"By the way, your birthday's October twenty-ninth, isn't it?"

"So?"

"Here's your belated astrological prediction," McShane said, unfolding the paper in his pocket.

"Too bad you didn't see it first. Might have saved you and a lot of people some grief."

"Huh?"

"Let's be sure we do this right," McShane said. He went to the door and called to Royce's secretary. "Please come in here, miss."

She rose from her desk and walked into the office.

"Witness this, will you," he said, and went around the desk, taking his handcuffs out as he approached the attorney.

"Robert Royce, you have the right to remain silent . . ."

Epilogue

The store owner told him the only kosher wine he had in stock read KOSHER FOR PASSOVER. McShane blamed himself for not thinking about bringing something until the last moment. There wasn't all that much choice in Parksville. It was either this or go back to Liberty, and he was already late.

"What does that mean?" he asked.

"Passover? It's a Jewish holiday."

"When was it?"

"I don't know. Some time back in April."

"April!"

"What's the difference? This stuff don't go bad."

McShane considered.

"All right, I'll take it," he said.

A few minutes later he pulled into the Golds' driveway. The first snow had fallen in the Catskills a week before, and it had remained near freezing ever since. Leafless tree limbs were coated with ice, and a fine crust of stale snow coated the ground and the yards. Harry Gold, back on his feet, had shoveled and swept his walkway clear.

Two days earlier Anna Gold had been released from the hospital and was home recuperating. She and her father had effected a cease-fire and begun a painfully slow reconciliation, each extracting the smallest compromises from the other. McShane had visited Anna a number of times at the hospital but had spent most of his visit talking quietly with Miriam in the waiting room. He had also had some conversation with Harry Gold and had discovered, to his surprise, that the man was a football fan.

"I don't watch on Saturday," Harry emphasized, "but I watch on Sunday."

It turned out he was a Giants fan too, and he was anxiously looking forward to the Super Bowl. The Giants were playing today and Harry had invited him.

"My father's not in a good mood," Miriam said when she greeted McShane at the front door. "Someone important is not able to play today."

"Gordon, knee injury," McShane said. "But Foster's good backup."

"*You* tell him," she said. He smiled.

"How's Anna?"

"She's good. Waiting to see you. She wants to know what you found out about that name on the wall."

"Oh." He stopped smiling. She pressed her lips together and shook her head in anticipation.

Anna was in the living room, reading a magazine. She was lying on the settee, a blanket over her. The moment she saw McShane her face brightened.

"How are you doing?" he asked her.

"Good," she said. "You told me you would have information for me today," she reminded him. He looked at Miriam and then back at Anna.

"Do you think it's good to keep thinking about all this?" he asked gently.

"No, but I've got to face the horror and conquer it on my own," she said. McShane smiled.

"Yes, there were two other victims, and yes, the name on the wall belonged to a teenage girl. We dug up her remains in the backyard. From what Dunbar said, it appears she induced her own miscarriage to get them to let her go."

Anna nodded.

"I almost knew it all just from being in that room."

"It's over, Anna. Bury it," McShane advised.

She smiled.

"I will."

"My father is waiting in the den," Miriam said.

"Oh. Good. I . . . er, picked this up without realizing it was kosher for Passover," he said, handing her the bag with the bottle of wine. "Hope it's still good."

"It'll be good on Passover next," Miriam replied with a twinkle in her eye. "Go." She took the wine from him and he crossed the hall to the den, where Harry Gold sat glaring at the television.

"Ah, Mr. Detective, you hear about Gordon?"

"Yeah, but Foster—"

"He doesn't hold up under pressure. You'll see. They'll collapse in the fourth quarter again."

McShane laughed.

"Sit. Miriam, you're watching the turkey? It's important it's moist."

"I know how to make turkey, Papa."

"You ever have a kosher turkey, Mr. Detective?"

"I don't know."

"If you did, you'd remember. It has a better taste."

"I still don't understand this kosher thing," McShane said.

"Miriam, the man needs something to drink. For you," he said, "we have some of that beer."

"Thank you," he said. Miriam laughed and went for it.

"So, you don't understand kosher. Where was I last time? Oh, yes: The Jewish dietary laws prescribed are not only a diet for the body but a diet for the soul, to maintain one's spiritual well-being." He paused to turn, his long, thick right forefinger up. "You must not be afraid of sacrifice, Mr. Detective."

"Papa," Miriam said, returning with a can and a glass, "you're lecturing him again."

"What lecturing? He asks questions, I answer."

"Answer, but don't lecture."

Harry raised his eyebrows.

"I guess, even in my own house, I've got to be politically correct," he said.

And they laughed.

It was almost time for the kickoff. McShane sat back. He couldn't help feeling he was a stranger in a strange land, visiting another country, but for a long time now he had been wandering, a man without a country, a man whom Cookie had rightfully accused of being without faith. It was good to be someplace where there was faith without being threatened by it. Harry Gold wasn't trying to convert him, wasn't going to picket his home or his place of business, wasn't going to threaten to withhold votes or boycott products. He would explain himself and his belief and then live and let live. His faith fortified him, and he was not to be condemned for that.

Why there had to be all these differences between people, McShane did not know. When he gazed at Miriam Gold, he saw her gazing back and he imagined she wondered about the same thing. It was a question that would take time to answer; it was a question that might never be answered, but it was a good question to ask and ask.

So many things abducted us in our lives and took us away from the basic truths, the basic good, he thought. He had made a contribution toward stopping it, and Cookie had been right: It had given him a renewed sense of purpose and built his self-confidence. It was good to be alive and working and fighting the good fight.

The cheers went up on the television screen.

"You know that's a pigskin, Papa," Miriam Gold teased. Harry raised his eyebrows.

From the other room came the wonderful melodic sound of Anna Gold's laughter.